Reclaimed

REBECCA MARTIN
ILLUSTRATED BY JOYCE HANSEN

© Carlisle Press May 2019
All rights reserved. No portion of this book may be reproduced by any means, electronic or mechanical, including photocopying, recording, or by any information storage retrieval system, without written permission of the copyright owner, except for the inclusion of brief quotations for a review.

ISBN: 978-1-933753-79-9

Rebecca Martin
Illustrated by: Joyce Hansen
Book Design by: Larisa Yoder
Printed in the USA by Carlisle Printing of Walnut Creek

Carlisle Press
WALNUT CREEK

2673 Township Road 421
Sugarcreek, Ohio 44681
phone | 800.852.4482

Author's Introduction to the

Eastward Trails Trilogy

Who are the Russian Mennonites? Their roots go back to Holland, where, in the 1530s, God raised up a church to follow Him in simplicity and surrender. These Anabaptist "heretics" were persecuted severely. Many of them migrated eastward to Poland and Prussia. In *Reclaimed*, the first book, the author uses fictional characters to tell the story of flight from Holland to Poland.

However, the Russian Mennonites' roots are not only Dutch. In *Eva's Milk Pail* (Fall 2020), the second book, you will find families of Anabaptist believers leaving Germany because of persecution. They seek safety in Austria, Moravia, and Czechoslovakia. Everywhere there is persecution. Eventually they flee Poland and join the brethren there.

Many years pass. When the Polish-Prussian government becomes too repressive, the Mennonites move on to Russia. That happens in the 1700s. For about 140 years they prosper in Russia.

In *Trail Breaker* (Winter 2020), the third book, you will meet families who are dealing with the chaos of civil war and communism in the Russia of 1918 to 1920. Throughout the three books, major happenings are based on historical fact.

History, Geography, Social Studies, Politics, Religion—all must be taken into account when recreating a setting from the past. This story tries to present a picture of Europe in the 1530s, based on facts gleaned from *Martyrs Mirror* and encyclopedias. However, the main characters with their thoughts, feelings, and actions are fictional.

The following are actual place names appearing in the story: Amsterdam, Leeuwarden, Münster, Gdansk (Danzig), Vistula River, Skagerrak, Kattegat, Friesland, Netherlands, Denmark, Norway, Poland, Baltic Sea, North Sea.

Titles in the
Eastward Trails Trilogy

Eva's Milk Pail
not actual cover

Second in the series
Coming Fall 2020

Trail Breaker
not actual cover

Third in the series
Coming Winter 2020

People in This Story Who Actually lived

Balthasar Hubmaier
Conrad Grebel
Felix Manz
Wilhelm Rueblin
Michael Sattler
King Ferdinand
King Sigismund
Emperor Charles
Obbe Phillips
Münsterites
Teutonic Knights
Luther
Zwingli
Magellan
Matthias Lang
Provost Aichele
Simon Stumpf
Thomas Müntzer

Table of Contents

Author's Introduction iii
War Against the Sea 1
From the Sewers 5
The Boys, Too 10
More Questions 14
Münsterites 18
Bells in the Night 22
Up From the Marsh 27
Meeting in a Barn 32
A Walk With Lisa 37
Marpeck's Story 41
Discovered! 46
The Emperor's Decree 51
On the Move 56
Setting Sail 60
On the Shoals 64
Freed 68
Home in the Hay 72
Found Out! 76
Capture 80
Strong Rock 85
Cleft of the Rock 89
Not Far From the Kingdom 94
Gdansk Harbor 98
Almost Home 102
Interrogation 106
Offscourings 110
Ice Dam 115
Incorruptible Seed 120
Lisa, Too 124

Chapter One

War Against the Sea

A stiff breeze blew in from the North Sea. It sent the great wooden arms of the windmills spinning in a brisk flap-flap-flap tempo. On days when the wind was low, the arms revolved with a mere lazy flap…flap…flap. But today, Bettje would have been hard-pressed to keep time with a hammer.

Hurrying along the top of a dike, Bettje and her brother drew closer to a towering windmill. Its whole structure creaked and groaned under the tremendous power of the wind. "You know," said Bettje laughingly, "I could almost picture this windmill plunging away over the polders, as though its arms were sails."

"Such talk!" snorted Jan, who at seventeen had little use for his sister's fancies. "So you would change this polder* back into a sea, and have the windmills sail around upon it like ships!"

Far from dampening Bettje's imagination, this gruff statement only enhanced it. She clasped her hands in delight, gazing across the flat green fields all dotted with windmills. "What a nice picture!

---
* low lying land reclaimed from the sea

Every windmill a ship, and the fields a sea!"

Jan reached up and grabbed his hat as a gust threatened to tear it from his head. "Don't forget—only a few hundred years ago, that is exactly what you would have seen while looking across this very space. A long arm of the North Sea used to curve in here, all the way to Leeuwarden. Our city was once a seaport on a bay called the Middlezee!"

"I know," said Bettje, glancing now toward the walled city to the east. "Father has told us the story many times of how this polder was reclaimed from the sea back in the twelve and thirteen hundreds. Just think how hard people must have worked to do that!"

Jan nodded. "Back-breaking work, to be sure. First they had to dig hundreds of ditches to drain the water back into the North Sea. They had to build dikes. And ever since then, people have been working hard to keep the water out."

"It's true, isn't it?" agreed Bettje. "That's why Father is a dike reeve on the board of the Water Authorities. Our country is always waging war against the sea."

Gazing westward, Bettje shivered. Somewhere beyond the dark line of the horizon, mighty waves from the North Sea pounded against the dikes. "I always find it a wee bit scary," she admitted, "to think we live on land that's actually lower than the sea. Only the dikes keep the water from sweeping in over us!"

"The city itself is higher than the polders," Jan reminded her. "As long as we're at home in our own house we needn't fear flooding."

The pair now left the dike and traveled up the road toward the walls of Leeuwarden. "I'm glad you're with me," Bettje said. "Those guards at the city gates give me the creeps. They act so suspicious! As though they suspect ordinary teenagers of being criminals."

"It didn't used to be this way," Jan observed. "I remember when we could pass freely in and out of the city without being questioned at all."

Glancing around to ensure no one was nearby, Bettje confided, "I think it's because of the Anabaptists—those horrid people who refuse to obey the church. The city authorities want to make sure there are no Anabaptists in Leeuwarden."

"I can't see why anyone would dare to become an Anabaptist. Not after what the authorities did to Andrew Claessen in March," Jan said.

This brought another shudder for Bettje. "I wish you hadn't mentioned it. I've spent weeks trying to forget that."

"Well, it happened, so you probably won't be able to forget it completely," came Jan's cryptic reply.

Nearing the city gate, they fell silent. A soldier in a red jerkin peered at them from beneath his metal helmet. "Name and address?" he demanded.

Jan spoke up sturdily. "Jan and Bettje, children of Adrian Weaver. Address, 46 Benstrasse."

"You're going home then?"

Jan nodded. Bettje found herself wanting to smile. Only a few hours ago this same soldier had questioned them when they left the city. Yet he acted as though he had never seen them before.

"What was your business out of town?" barked the soldier.

"We took a message from Mother to her brother, our Uncle Leonhard." This information, too, Jan had given a few hours ago.

"All right, you may go in," conceded the soldier, sounding as reluctant as if he suspected them of being thieves.

Under his breath, Jan said to his sister as they hurried along the narrow street, "He makes me feel like a villain."

"And yet we're children of a respected citizen; one of the dike reeves at that," Bettje added indignantly.

Jan shook his head slowly. "It seems like they don't dare trust anybody anymore. Andrew Claessen was a respected citizen too, in the village of Drourijp. And yet he got tangled up with those horrible

Anabaptists. They can deceive anybody, the way it appears."

"Oh, there you go talking about Anabaptists again," Bettje reproached him. "I'm so glad we're home now." Running on ahead of him, she wrenched open the door of their house, which was a tall half-timbered structure wedged tightly between other buildings. What a good feeling it was to be greeted by Mother's smile!

Chapter Two

From the Sewers

Hardly had Jan and Bettje closed the door behind them when a thunderous knock sounded. "Adrian Weaver! Open to the Water Authorities!" a gruff voice sounded through the wooden door.

"Shall I open, Mother?" asked Jan, who always felt responsible when Father was away.

"Yes, please." For some reason, Mother's face beneath her frilly white cap had gone pale.

But Bettje relaxed when she saw who was on the doorstep. It was only Heinrich, another of the dike reeves. "Where is your father?" he immediately asked Jan.

"He is away on a business trip to some German cities," Jan replied.

"Ah, that Adrian. He is such a driven man," said Heinrich with a shake of his head. "Why, just his wages as a dike reeve would be more money than most men make. But not content with that, he is also in the weaving business, selling fabrics all over Europe." Heinrich's tone betrayed his admiration for such an enterprising man.

Then he continued, "But if it happens too often that Adrian is not at home to fulfill his duties as a water authority, maybe he will lose that position. There is trouble with the northeast dike. The sea has been very rough this past week. We wanted Adrian to come and have a look."

Bettje suppressed a gasp. No child of the Netherlands could miss the warning if the words "trouble" and "dike" were mentioned in a single breath.

"Are there leaks?" Mother asked in concern.

"Some, yes. And also the potential for a major break. Parts of that dike are old—too old for the pounding it gets. The Water Authority is considering some replacement work for this year." Heinrich had a pompous way of speaking, as though he felt sure what he had to say was very important. "When did you say Adrian will be back?"

"I don't know," Mother admitted. "Within a week, I think."

Heinrich muttered darkly, "I wish he were here now. We need him to help make decisions."

"I'm sorry," said Mother.

"What good is an apology?" snapped Heinrich as he turned to go. "As soon as Adrian gets home, tell him he's to report to the Water Authority."

"I'll do that," Mother promised.

Bettje stood anxiously twisting her hands. Though fifteen years old, at such a time those little-girl fears still gnawed at her. "What if the dikes break?" she whispered hoarsely.

"I told you. Leeuwarden's higher up than the polders," Jan reminded her.

"Yes—but the villages—so many people live right in the path of the sea, if it were to break through the dikes." Already Bettje could picture a dark wall of water rolling over the polders, destroying everything in its path.

Jan let out a derisive chuckle. "I thought you said it would be a pretty sight to have the windmills floating like ships on water."

"I didn't really mean that," Bettje denied. "Oh, I hope Father comes home soon. He'll know how to repair the dikes."

"He has helped with many repairs," Mother agreed quietly. "Bettje, if you will make supper I'll do some more weaving."

"All right," agreed Bettje. She prepared a pot of leek-and-potato soup and carried it to the hearth. Alarming thoughts jostled each other in her mind. Leaking dikes…Anabaptists infiltrating the city… why, danger lurked everywhere!

That very evening, something happened to increase twofold Bettje's thoughts of danger. She and Mother and Jan had each retired to their upstairs bedrooms. Bettje was almost dozing off when she became aware of a low, insistent sound from downstairs.

Somebody was tapping on the door! Not the street door, but the one that opened onto the back alley. How strange!

Bettje lay frozen with dread. Had Mother heard the sound? What if thieves awaited, out there in the darkness?

She heard a rustling in the hall. Then Mother's footsteps. Outside Jan's door she paused. "Jan. Will you go down with me? Someone is at the door."

There was Jan now, thumping down the stairs after Mother. Jan was so brave. Lying in the darkness, Bettje asked herself, *When will I ever learn to be brave like him?*

She heard the back door being opened, then strange voices. Somebody was crying. It sounded like a small child!

Bettje leaped out of bed. She simply had to know what was going on down there.

One candle flickered in the kitchen. Bettje blinked in amazement. Four strangers huddled near the door—and three of them were girls, younger than herself! The fourth was an infant held in the arms of the tallest girl. Bettje could not see whether the ragged bundle was a boy or a girl, but pitiful crying rose from its folds.

"We've been hiding in the sewers," the tallest girl faltered.

The sewers! Suddenly Bettje became aware of a foul odor. Unmistakably the odor of the sewers, those dank underground passages beneath Leeuwarden, meant to carry away waste water. Bettje drew back in disgust.

But Mother did not. Instead, she stepped forward and took the bundle. "Is the child sick?"

"We think so. That's why we had to come out of hiding. Somebody...somebody said you might help us." Misery and fear haunted the girl's eyes.

Carefully, Mother unwrapped the bundle. "Bettje, please heat some water. And the leftover soup, too."

Sullenly, Bettje poked the fire to life. Mother was actually going to let these awful-smelling people stay!

"You may sit there on the bench," Mother said to the girls. She began offering spoonfuls of warm water to the child. The whimpering stopped.

Finally Mother asked the question that Bettje was wondering about. "Where are your parents?"

The oldest girl swallowed hard. The next one said in a hollow voice, "They are both dead."

The tallest girl coughed. When she spoke, it seemed she had to force out the words. "We are Andrew Claessen's children."

Bettje almost dropped the pot of soup. Andrew Claessen! The wicked Anabaptist who had been executed in March! Somehow it had never occurred to Bettje that he could have been a father with children.

"Mother died two years ago," the second girl said. "When Mary was born." She pointed to the child in Mother's arms. "There are seven of us. Our three brothers said we must go for help."

"And they are still in the sewers?" Mother asked sharply.

"Sometimes. They go out and work, too. We needed money for food."

"Nobody should have to live in the sewers," Mother declared.

Bettje held her breath. Was she going to tell Jan to find those three boys and bring them in as well?

To her relief, Mother said instead, "Jan, you go on up to bed. These girls need baths. Is the water warming up, Bettje? Oh, and please get some of your outgrown dresses. In the chest beyond the stairs."

Bettje did as she was told. But all the while she was screaming inwardly, "These are Anabaptist children! They shouldn't be in our house! They will only bring us trouble!"

And yet—and yet; when Bettje poured water for the girls' baths and saw their misery and pain, she could understand why Mother was doing this. What else could she do?

Chapter Three

The Boys, Too

Somehow, Mother found room for three of the girls in the guest bedroom. She took the little one into her own bedroom. Several times during the night, Bettje heard her thin wailing.

At breakfast time the next morning, none of the elder three were astir. "They must be exhausted. Let them sleep," said Mother, who was busy feeding the little one. Bettje had to admit that Mary looked decidedly cute. How hungrily she ate the porridge! Before long she grabbed the spoon away from Mother and began feeding herself.

"She doesn't really seem sick anymore," Mother observed. "Maybe she was simply hungry. Is that right, Mary? Were you hungry?"

The child looked up with big blue eyes. First she nodded, and then she smiled—such a pretty baby smile!

Bettje sat there watching the little girl eat. After a while she asked, "But Mother, what will happen if people find out that we are sheltering the children of an Anabaptist?"

Mother gave her a long look. "Who would harm us for showing

kindness to these poor children?"

Bettje shrugged. "I don't know. But Anabaptists are very wicked."

"Why do you say that?" Mother asked quietly.

Bettje was startled. "Well, you know they are wicked, don't you? They do not obey the church."

When Mother did not reply, Jan spoke up. "Just because the father was wicked doesn't mean the children are too."

Meanwhile, Mary had finished eating. Mother wiped her face, then put her down on the floor.

Bettje watched her curiously. So far, someone had always carried the child. Could Mary walk? Was she strong enough?

Mary took a few hesitant steps. Seeming to gather courage, she moved faster. Soon she was walking around the kitchen like any normal toddler.

The other three girls looked a little sheepish as they filed downstairs. Bettje had learned that their names were Carla, Lela and Anneken, but she was not sure which was which.

When the three had also eaten, Mother asked, "Can you tell us where to find your brothers?"

Alarm flickered in the oldest girl's eyes. Lela, the second girl, replied, "Over on the next street is a sort of bridge. If you look down below, you can see where we went in and out of the sewers. We never went far in there."

Mother prompted gently, "This place where you stayed—was it dry?"

Carla, the oldest, replied, "Yes, it was dry. There was a beam above the sewage where we could sit and lie down."

Bettje shuddered inwardly. This girl sounded grateful—for what? A spot in the sewers where they had been safe and dry.

"We can go back there now," Carla offered swiftly. "It looks like Mary is feeling better."

"No, no!" protested Mother. "You do not have to go back into the sewers. And we hope to find a home for your brothers too. Jan, please come here!"

He appeared from the back, where he had been working at the loom.

"I have been thinking about the girls' brothers. Surely Bernhard and Elizabeth would take them in. Would you go and ask them about it? And if Bernhard agrees, ask him also to go with you to find the boys."

"Yes, Mother." Jan reached immediately for his cap. Since Bernhard lived only a few doors down the street, Jan was back soon, with Bernhard at his side. "Now where did you say we can find those boys?"

Though Carla seemed hesitant about speaking to this latest stranger, she managed to explain where the sewer entrance could be found. "Of course, I do not know whether the boys are there. They may be out looking for food, or for work."

"We'll find them," Bernhard said confidently.

After he and Jan had gone, Carla asked, "Did you say you have a loom? I have experience with weaving, and I surely would like to work for you if you keep us."

"We have several looms. Carla, how old are you?" Mother asked curiously.

"I'm almost sixteen."

"Then you're older than I am!" exclaimed Bettje.

Carla smiled. "I'm not very big. But I like weaving."

"So do I," said Bettje. "Shall we work on the looms now, Mother?"

"Certainly. I'll help you get started."

Mother watched Carla for a few minutes. Then she said warmly, "I can see that you're good at it, Carla."

"Better than I am," lamented Bettje, watching Carla's flying shuttle.

"Weaving is what we did at our house," Carla explained quietly. "Even Lela has done quite a bit of it."

"Maybe we will have to set up a third loom," Mother suggested. "Woolen goods are in great demand; we can never make too much."

Shortly afterwards, Jan returned—alone. Bettje asked, "You didn't find the boys?" To her own surprise, she felt disappointed. What mixed-up feelings these Claessen children brought her! One moment she hated them for being Anabaptists; and the next moment she liked them, because they really were just ordinary people like herself.

Jan grinned. "We found them, all right. They were just coming out of the entrance. When they saw us, they ducked back in, but Bernhard soon convinced them that we meant no harm."

"Will they come here to visit us?" Anneken asked eagerly.

"Yes, but first they're going to have baths and put on some clean clothes," Jan told the child.

Bettje marveled at the note of tenderness in her brother's voice. Helping these needy children was bringing out a side of Jan that she barely knew.

And maybe the same is true of me, Bettje thought wryly.

Chapter Four

More Questions

It was amazing how well the four girls blended into the Weaver household. After a few days, Bettje felt as though they were her sisters. True, most of the time they were quiet and rather sad—which was no wonder, considering what they had been through. But they were friendly and always ready to speak when spoken to.

On Saturday, Bettje and Carla once again worked companionably at the looms, while the younger three played nearby. "I suppose you'll go to church with us tomorrow," Bettje commented.

Carla's eyes widened. "I—I'm afraid we can't do that."

"We could just tell folks that you're friends visiting from the country," Bettje suggested, thinking that Carla must fear discovery.

"It's not that." Carla sounded troubled.

Skilfully guiding her shuttle, Bettje waited in silence. Though she didn't want to pressure Carla, she really wondered what other reason Carla would give for not attending church.

"I guess you know why my father was put to death?" Carla asked.

"He and Mother taught us that many of the Catholic beliefs are wrong. Like those images in the churches. Father said God's Word forbids such things."

Bettje's shuttle dropped unheeded to her lap. "So you're saying you girls are also Anabaptists, like your parents?"

Pain washed over Carla's face. "I have not yet received the true baptism. But two of my brothers have. I am sorry if this offends you."

"I—I don't know what to think," Bettje mumbled. Desperately she longed for a word alone with Mother.

So when Mother announced that she was going to the market, Bettje jumped at the chance to go along. As soon as the two of them were out of sight from the house, Bettje grabbed Mother's arm and hissed, "Did you know that those girls are—are corrupted with Anabaptist beliefs?"

Mother took several steps in silence. When she spoke, she measured her words carefully. "Bettje, perhaps you don't realize that there are several—ah—branches of Anabaptism. You've heard us talking about Melchior Hofmann's followers, and how deceived they are. But Bettje, there are also Anabaptists who follow God's Word in truth."

Bettje reeled back as though Mother had struck her a blow. Never had she dreamed that her own dear mother would speak a good word for those heretics! "But Mother—they don't obey the church. They don't baptize their babies. With my own ears I've heard the bishop saying that Anabaptists are doomed to hell."

"Oh, Bettje!" There was anguish in Mother's voice now. "You are causing me to say things that I would rather not say until—until Father gets back. Please, let's talk about something else. But remember this, Bettje: we must never close our hearts to the truth of God."

Miserably, Bettje walked on in silence. She felt too mixed up to speak at all, whether about Anabaptists or anything else. Whatever had come over Mother? She actually sounded as though she sympathized with Carla!

But that could not be. It simply could not be. Anabaptists were wicked heretics who deserved to die—yes, deserved a horrible death like Andrew Claessen's.

However, since Bettje was used to expressing her feelings, she said after awhile, "I wish we'd never laid eyes on those Claessen girls."

"Oh, but someone had to help them," Mother insisted.

"I mean—I mean, if they start infecting our family with these heretical ideas, then I wish they'd just leave." Bettje knew she was dangerously close to the subject Mother had asked her to drop.

"They are not infecting us," Mother said sternly—so sternly that Bettje got the message. She really had to stop talking about these things!

But she couldn't resist saying belligerently, "I don't like all these unanswered questions."

Mother's tone softened. "I know. I'm only asking you to wait till Father gets back. Then we will try to help you with your questions."

By the time they reached the market, Bettje had recovered from her grumpiness. She had always enjoyed the sights, smells and sounds of this busy spot where the farmers sold their produce.

Another thing Bettje had always enjoyed was going to church, so the next morning she set off eagerly with Mother and Jan. The cathedral's soaring spires and lofty tower gave her such an exalted feeling. Inside, the vast domed ceilings with their exquisite carvings, and the tall stained-glass windows, all contributed to a sense of hushed holiness.

Even though Bettje understood very little of what the priest said—he spoke mostly in Latin—it made her feel good to hear him. After all, was not the priest God's messenger to the people?

Partway through the service, Bettje found herself eyeing the images of Mary, of Jesus, and of the saints. What had Carla said? "God's Word forbids such things."

But how could a mere girl like Carla know? Or how could her father, an unlettered weaver, know? Ordinary people didn't read God's Word. They couldn't. It was in Latin. Ordinary people didn't know Latin.

Walking homeward with Mother and Jan, Bettje remarked, "It's strange to think there'll be four people in our house when we arrive."

"Seven," Jan corrected her. "The Claessen boys plan to come over from Bernhards' place."

"Oh," said Bettje. It seemed to her that Jan had been spending a lot of time with those boys. Did he realize that two of them had received a second baptism?

Just as they mounted the steps at home, the door opened and a man and a woman came out. "I hope you don't mind that we kept the young people company while you were gone," the man apologized hurriedly.

To Bettje, the man was a stranger. But Mother evidently knew him. Calmly she answered, "No, we don't mind. Thank you."

Questions bubbled up inside Bettje. She could not keep them to herself. "Was that an Anabaptist?" she demanded.

Mother's reply was evasive. "It could have been."

"Ever since the Claessen girls came," Bettje went on in a rush, "I've wondered about something. They said that 'someone' suggested we might give them refuge. Who was that someone? Could it have been that man?"

"It could have been," Mother said again. Her voice also held a warning note—and Bettje knew why. "Wait till Father comes home, then we will explain." Those were her unspoken words.

Reaching for the door latch, Bettje thought stormily, *It seems to me there's quite a bit of explaining to do. Why would an Anabaptist suggest to Anabaptist children that* we *might take them in?*

What in the world was going on?

More Questions   17

Chapter Five

Münsterites

Early in the week, a storm blew up. Rain drummed on the roof and wind gusted down the street. When Jan came inside, dripping wet from the rain, he announced, "I had to bend nearly double in order to make headway against the wind."

Bettje's thoughts flew immediately to the North Sea. One stormy day last year, she had stood watching the relentless onslaught of breakers against the dikes. A fury of foam billowed up as the waves crashed, battering this barrier that prevented them from rolling over the land. The North Sea in a storm was a fearsome sight. "I hope the Water Authorities managed to repair those dikes," she said tremulously.

Only a few minutes later, Heinrich's coarse voice came through the door. "Open, Adrian Weaver!"

Instantly, the four Claessen girls melted to the back room. From there, Bettje knew, they would steal noiselessly down the stairs into the cellar, just as they had been taught to do whenever visitors came.

Heinrich blustered in, using a handkerchief to wipe his streaming hair and face. "What a day!" he puffed, and then his eyes darted around the room. "Adrian still not home?"

"No." Mother's voice faltered. "Something must have detained him."

Like a blow to the stomach, a realization hit Bettje. Maybe something had happened to Father! Maybe that was why he had not returned!

"Well, he should hurry and get back. We need him. We've been so busy repairing dikes that we barely have time to eat and sleep anymore," Heinrich growled. "When he gets home, tell him to report immediately to the Water Authorities."

When Mother had once again promised to do that, Heinrich let out a gusty sigh. "This city is beset with many kinds of danger. There is always the danger of the sea, and now we also have those Anabaptists threatening to over run the land! It is enough to make a man quake in his shoes."

Heinrich moved closer to the fire, evidently hoping to dry his clothes at least a little before plunging out into the rain again. "Why, over in the German city of Münster, the Anabaptists have taken control of the government! They forced all the citizens to be baptized, and claim that Münster is the New Jerusalem."

He coughed and waited, as though expecting Jan or Mother to say something. When no one spoke he continued. "Münster is under siege right now. The Bishop's troops are camped outside the city, and they say people are dying of starvation inside the walls. At least one of the heretic leaders has been executed. Those Anabaptists will find out that the church is sovereign and must not be disobeyed!"

"I am sorry to hear of such things," Mother said.

Heinrich went on. "You might think, that is way over in Münster; surely no such things will happen here. But there are all too many Anabaptists in the Netherlands. Surely you heard what happened near Bolsward just this past March?"

"We heard very little," Mother said.

"Why, some of those Münsterites, or whatever you call them, took possession of a monastery and barricaded themselves against the royal soldiers! But by the end of March, the royal troops had overpowered the villains. I don't know how many people were put to death." Heinrich licked his lips. "We will show these Anabaptists who is boss!"

He took a few steps toward the door. "You know, I have often wondered why people would risk their lives like these heretics do. And I think I've figured out why. The people of the Netherlands hate to be under the rule of Spain. They hate it that the Holy Roman Emperor is Charles, the Spanish king. So they recklessly hope to throw off the yoke of Spain, using fanatic religion to lure people into their ranks. Don't you think that might be the reason?" He peered at Mother, once again waiting for an answer.

She hesitated. "I don't understand these things."

"Well, I believe that's the reason. And so the Holy Roman Church must suffer because of these misguided rebels. I hope we can soon rid the land of them all," blustered Heinrich as he went out the door.

Bettje sat there with clenched fists. "Mother, it makes me wonder why we dare to keep the Claessen girls here. To think that their parents were such rebels!"

"Ah, Bettje," said Mother—and there she stopped. Going to the head of the cellar stairs, she told the fugitives, "You may come up now."

Slowly they re-entered the kitchen. Lela said unsteadily, "We could hear what the man said. We just wanted to tell you that our father was not one of those—those Münsterites."

Carla put in, "We are taught that the followers of Jesus do not use the sword."

"Then who is your leader if it is not this Melchior Hofmann who started the Münsterite sect?" Jan wanted to know.

"Obbe Phillips is our minister," Carla replied. Then she added hastily, "Perhaps I should not have said that. I do not want to endanger Obbe."

"You can trust us," Mother assured her.

Bettje frowned. These girls seemed so sure of themselves. And it almost seemed that Mother was on their side! It was all very baffling and mysterious.

Later, as the girls worked side by side at the loom, Bettje asked abruptly, "How can you be so sure you're right, Carla?"

The other girl fixed her blue eyes on Bettje. "I—I really don't consider myself right. I am just a sinner like you. Jesus is the One who is right. And in His Word He says He wants us to be His children."

Bettje sat dumbfounded. Never before had she heard anyone talking like this. Inwardly she fumed, *How dare she call me a sinner? I am a good Catholic. I take mass and make confessions. Whereas she—she is a follower of a radical cult that obeys neither pope nor emperor!*

Yet Carla's words seemed to burn a hole in Bettje's heart. "Jesus is the One who is right. And in His Word He says He wants us for His children."

With a little snort, Bettje sent her shuttle flying again. Sometimes she felt disgusted with these girls. Their serene, self-assured ways could be infuriating!

Chapter Six

Bells in the Night

From high on the city wall, Bettje could look down on the army camped below. Swords and spears gleamed. Armor flashed in the sun. Like a stream of molten lava, fear coursed through Bettje.

Now the soldiers were marching! They pushed toward the city gate, breaking through with a splintering crash.

Right inside the gate stood Father, trying singlehandedly to defend the city. But his puny sword fell from his hand, and he fell beneath the onslaught. A tide of soldiers flowed mercilessly over him.

"Father! Father!" cried Bettje, her voice choking.

Then she woke up. Relief was so profound that it left her trembling. "I guess it's no wonder I had such a dream," Bettje told herself with a shaky little laugh. "Not after all those Anabaptist stories Heinrich told us."

Rain still pounded on the roof. Suddenly, above the roar of the wind, Bettje heard a new sound. Bells! In the middle of the night, that could mean only one thing: an alarm!

Like any child of the Netherlands, Bettje's thoughts flew to the dikes. This storm must be putting tremendous pressure on them. Were they breaking? Were the bells a call to all able-bodied men to go out and fight the sea? Were the Water Authorities out there, desperately trying to barricade a breach with wooden beams and sand?

Bettje sat up in bed, listening. Would Jan hear the bells? Would he go to help?

Sure enough, in a few minutes she heard his bedroom door opening. Footsteps hustled down the stairs. Reaching for her beads, Bettje recited some prayers to the holy mother Mary. *If I cannot go out into the night to fight the sea, I can at least pray for the men's safety,* Bettje thought.

The bells clanged on. Each "bong" seemed to call, "More! More! We need more help to battle the sea."

Sleep would not return for Bettje. The wind and the rain kept up a steady roar. Realizing that Mother was down in the kitchen, Bettje decided to go there as well.

In the candlelight, Mother's face looked surprisingly calm. She sat at the table, her hands folded. "So you can't sleep either, Bettje?" she asked.

"No. The storm is so loud. And I'm worried about Jan. Oh, how I wish Father were here! He would know what to do about the leaking dikes."

"Surely the other reeves also know what needs to be done," Mother said. She closed her eyes, and her lips moved.

Was she praying? Bettje wondered. But how could she pray without her beads? Mother's rosary was nowhere in sight.

Soon the three eldest Claessen girls also appeared in the kitchen. Without a word they took seats near the table.

"The storm is so noisy that I didn't hear you coming," Mother commented.

Carla nodded. "It makes me think of a story Father told us from the Bible. About the time when Jesus was on the Sea of Galilee in a boat. The disciples were afraid they would perish!"

Mother's face lit up. "But when Jesus said, 'Peace, be still!' the storm stopped immediately."

Bettje stared at Mother. How did she know anything about this story from the Bible?

"Our parents taught us a song about that," Lela said.

"Could you sing it?" asked Mother.

The three girls looked shyly at one another. When Carla started singing, the others joined in. The simple little song sounded strangely peaceful against the raging background of the storm. Though Bettje did not understand all the words, again and again she caught the phrase, "Peace, be still. Peace, be still." She had never heard a song like that.

If only the real storm would stop. Restlessly, Bettje paced to the window. But there was only darkness beyond the rain-lashed glass.

After a while Mother suggested, "Maybe we should all go to bed and try sleeping again. Let's hope Jan comes home in time for breakfast."

In spite of the storm's thundering, Bettje did fall asleep. Some hours later she awoke to sunshine and stillness. Instantly she went to the window.

But of course, not much was to be seen from there. Buildings crowded close on every side. Below in the streets, only a few large puddles remained to tell of the storm's fury. *I wonder what I expected to see?* Bettje asked herself with a little chuckle. *Did I think Leeuwarden's streets would be half full of floodwater?*

If only she could see out beyond the city to the polders. Had the dikes broken? Was the land flooded by raging waters from the North Sea?

Bettje hurried downstairs and looked eagerly around the kitchen.

Her heart dropped. No Jan.

Along with the Claessen girls, Bettje and Mother ate in silence. Only Mary spoke. She had a knack for chatting with whatever lay at hand; this morning it was her porridge. Counting each spoonful, she announced triumphantly that she had eaten thirteen spoons of porridge.

"Hush! You can't even count right," Anneken retorted.

"I can so! There were thirteen," insisted Mary in a wounded tone. Since she had no younger siblings, Bettje found such little-girl squabbles fascinating. Even when her heart was filled with anxiety for Jan, and indeed for all the villages on the polders. "Mother, if I were to go up to the head of the street, I could see out through the city gate. May I go?"

Mother smiled slightly. "You wish to find out whether there is a flood. But how do you know the gates will be open?"

"I don't know. I'm just hoping."

"I guess you may go. But don't stay long."

"I won't."

To Bettje's surprise, Lela spoke up wistfully, "I'd like to go with you."

"Me too!" exclaimed Anneken, and then of course, Mary added her own echo of "Me too!"

"Well, I suppose it should be all right," Mother agreed uncertainly. "You girls don't get much fresh air."

Carla said confidently, "We can hope people aren't thinking about heretics this morning, what with the storm and the threat of breaking dikes."

Bettje wasn't sure how she felt about a walk up the street with these girls. Hopefully no passersby would start asking questions.

"I'll carry you, Mary," Carla offered. "We don't want to slow Bettje down."

Barefooted they splashed through the puddles. From the crest of

Bells in the Night   25

the street they could see to the gate, and sure enough it was open.

Bettje let out a sigh of relief. "The polders are not covered with water. Our men must have won their battle with the sea." Never had the green fields and windmills been such a welcome sight.

"I see a few lakes where none had been," Lela observed.

"Perhaps the dikes leaked some water. But not enough to wash away villages," Bettje said. "Say! That man coming in through the gate just now—it looks like Jan! And who is with him?"

Heart beating fast, Bettje squinted into the bright sunlight. It couldn't be…but it was! Father was walking along beside Jan!

Running toward him, Bettje exclaimed, "You came in time to help with the dikes!"

Father's weary face broke into a smile. "Yesterday evening I was tempted to stop for rest at an inn, but the storm urged me homeward."

Jan said, "When I got to the dikes, Father was already there, directing the work. Do you know what one of the reeves told me? He said, 'Your father saved the day.'"

"No, no," protested Father. "I didn't do any more than the others." Questioningly, his eyes went to Bettje's four companions. "And who are your friends?"

Bettje glanced around to make sure no one was within hearing distance. "Andrew Claessen's girls. You know what happened to their father. They live with us now."

What a mixture of feelings showed in Father's face when he heard that! Surprise—delight—concern—and questions. Perhaps questions most of all.

Now at last, Bettje thought contentedly as she walked homeward at Father's side, *all the questions will be answered.*

Chapter Seven

Up From the Marsh

To Bettje's disappointment, Father slept away most of his first day at home. In the evening she heard her parents talking for a long time. *When will my turn come?* Bettje wondered impatiently. *When can I ask my questions, and hear all about Father's trip?*

After breakfast the next morning Father looked at Mother and said, "We have so much to tell that we hardly knew where to begin. But we decided to tell first about the gift that started it all." So saying, he left the table and went to the chest on the far wall. Pushing aside the chest, he got down on his hands and knees as though hunting for something.

Bettje watched in bewilderment. What had Father meant by "the gift that started it all"? And whatever was he looking for?

Next Father slid back one of the floor tiles and reached down into an opening that Bettje had not even known was there. When he stood up, he was holding a book in his hands—a big, heavy book with gold lettering on the cover. Since Bettje had never learned to read, she did not know what the letters said.

"This is a Bible. God's holy Word," Father said in a tone of hushed awe as he placed it on the table.

"In Dutch?" Jan asked incredulously.

"Yes. Perhaps you didn't know that the Bible is being translated into many common languages these days. After centuries of ignorance about God's Word, men are once again finding out the truth!" Gladness filled Father's voice.

Bettje shrank back in horror. What would their priest say if he knew there was a Bible in this house—a Bible that Father could read? Bettje knew what the priests believed about the Bible. It was not meant for unlearned people. Only the priests and bishops were qualified to interpret it.

Jan, however, seemed more curious than disturbed. "Did you say someone gave you this Bible as a gift?"

"No. I bought it. But the Bible is a gift to mankind from God—the gift of His Word, to teach us the truth. Ah, the riches Mother and I have gleaned from this book! It has changed our hearts, just as it has changed the hearts of thousands who read it. All across Europe, the light of God's Word is breaking through the darkness of Romanism!"

Apalled, Bettje sat speechless. She could not believe her ears. Her own father, speaking thus about the Holy Roman Church!

"Mother and I have been longing to tell you, Jan and Bettje, about these wonderful changes. But we were afraid. There are mighty forces that oppose the truth. We did not want to put our family in danger." His eyes went apologetically to the Claessen girls. "We were being cowards, I know. But now—after all that has happened, and after all that I learned during my travels—we can no longer be silent."

Protest welled up inside Bettje. "But Father! You cannot mean that you—" She could not bring herself to utter the words.

He held up a hand. "Please, don't use language that slanders the true believers. Why speak of Anabaptists—of the twice-baptized?

There is no such thing as a second baptism. There is only one true baptism, after a person has turned to the Lord in repentance. And those who are thus baptized become brethren. Brethren in the body of Christ."

It was too much to take in. Feeling faint, Bettje sank back against the wall. She wanted to cover her ears and scream, "Don't talk like that! Don't say you sympathize with the Anabaptists!"

As for Jan, he still didn't look perturbed. Leaning forward, he suggested, "Tell us how you came to these realizations."

Father passed a hand across his brow. "I can hardly find words to describe it. The experience is so overwhelming… Perhaps I can tell it best by relating it to something we are all familiar with: the reclaiming of land from the sea."

He laid his hand on the Bible. "We see a picture of that in the Bible's very first story. When God created the earth, it was originally without form and void, covered with water and darkness. I picture it as a great marshy bog: land and water mixed together.

"But God said, 'Let there be light.' And He said, 'Let the dry land appear.' So instead of darkness there was light. And instead of marsh, there was rich, dry soil, ready to grow all the beautiful fruits of God's creation."

In spite of her distress, Bettje found Father's vivid description creeping into her soul. Yes, indeed, she could picture it—the earth like a vast bog being drained to become a fertile polder!

"From that very soil, God created man," Father went on. "And at first man's heart was like the life-sustaining soil of the earth: open to the seed of God's Word, able to bring forth fruits of righteousness.

"But man was a creature of choice. He chose to turn away from God. The heart of man became permeated with sin, like the water-permeated soil of a bog.

"Down through the centuries, God provided ways for the heart of man to be reclaimed from this sad state. God provided the law of righteousness and sacrifice. Through faith and obedience, man's heart could return to God.

"Then, 1500 years ago, God sent His Son to the earth. Into His body on the cross Jesus took the sin of mankind and put it to death, once and for all! Thus the church was born—the church of the redeemed, the reclaimed, those who by faith become part of the body of Christ.

"Over time, the church lost its purity. Like a boggy mixture of water and land, it became horribly mixed up with human politics. But God in His mercy has awakened many men who speak for the truth. Oh, the stories I heard as I traveled through the German cities! Stories of Luther, and of Zwingli, and a host of others who sought to rid the church of impurity. Yet many of their efforts fell short. Often there was still not the preaching of the real, full truth.

"Take for example the city of Basel in Switzerland. More than ten years ago, the Council there began introducing reforms to the church. Reformer pastors were allowed to preach in the city's pulpits. In fact, by 1529 the entire city was compelled to embrace the reforming ideas of Zwingli."

Bettje's mind reeled. Yes, she had sometimes heard bits and pieces about those reformers over in the Swiss and German cities. She had even heard of reformer pastors right here in the Netherlands. But she had never paid much attention, for to her they were all "heretics" against the holy church.

Father continued. "Yet somehow, the people of Basel did not show much interest in this forced reformation. No real change took place in the corrupt lives of the people. For in Basel as also here in the Netherlands, church people often lived very wickedly.

"But only the full truth can free people from sin. Ministers of the truth—such as George Blaurock and Conrad Winkler—visited Basel. People's hearts were opened to the light. Here and there, as we might say, the 'dry land appeared,' ready for the bearing of truly righteous fruits. Hans Ludi became the minister for this little group.

Enraged that these so-called Anabaptists were gaining a foothold in the city, the Council of Basel put Ludi to death. Executed him with a sword in the marketplace, where all could see."

A hush fell over the kitchen. Bettje hardly dared look at Carla and Lela. What memories this must evoke for them!

Indeed, there were tears in the girls' eyes. But their faces remained upturned in rapt attention, eagerly waiting for Father to continue.

"Perhaps the authorities of Basel hoped this cruel act would squash the brethren. But the opposite was true! The martyrdom of Hans Ludi brought great spiritual awakening to the countryside.

"And this has been the case all across the German lands. The blood of the martyrs, far from extinguishing God's work, has been a means of mightily advancing it. When I think of the brethren in the German lands, I can't help it—I think of beautiful, dry polders rising up from a bog, ready to bring forth the fruits of righteousness."

Father's eyes lingered on Jan and Bettje. "So children, I hope you can understand what Mother and I are trying to say. You see, our own hearts were also a picture of sin and impurity, like a stagnant, evil-smelling bog. But in God's Word we can read this message to the believers: 'Ye are God's husbandry.' We are His farm, His polders. In our hearts, too, God can cause the 'dry land' to appear, and the fruits of righteousness to grow.

"And I ask you, Jan and Bettje, can such a thing prosper if it is kept hidden through shame and fear? Because that is what Mother and I have been doing with our faith. We have kept it hidden out of fear of the authorities, fear of suffering a martyrs' death.

"We can no longer do that. Jesus has given us light. Light cannot be hidden. We must go forth, trusting in Him, willing to receive His baptism, willing to suffer with Him. There is no other way."

For Bettje, the words dropped like a knell of doom. "There is no other way." Could she grasp it?

Yes, her questions had been answered. But now she was faced with this stark, terrible truth: her own parents were becoming Anabaptists.

Chapter Eight

Meeting in a Barn

It was horrible. Simply horrible. When Sunday came, Father said they would not be going to church. "We cannot, because in truth there is no such thing like 'going to church.' The church is not a building. It is the body of believers, saved by faith in the blood of the Lamb."

Whenever he said such things, Bettje tried to close her ears. She even tried to close her ears when he read aloud from the Bible. But it was hard. The things he said and the things he read were so powerful, so compelling!

"We will have a church meeting right here in this house," Father went on to say.

"How can you hold a meeting if nobody comes?" Bettje wondered.

"The believers will come. Bernhard and Elizabeth. The Claessen boys. Your Uncle Leonhards. And there are others."

Once again, Bettje found herself reeling as from a rain of blows. All those familiar people—and Father was saying they had become

Anabaptists!

"I'm going to church," Bettje declared.

"Ah, Bettje," said Mother sadly.

"Don't 'Ah, Bettje' me! I'm not going to be a heretic," she stormed.

"If the Claessen boys are coming, I'm staying here," Jan said.

Momentarily, Bettje wavered. Jan, too? Would he blindly follow Father and Mother? Then she, at least, must stay true to the mother church. "I'll go to church," she repeated. She longed for the familiar comfort of the stately cathedral, and of the friends she would meet there.

Bolstered by indignation, Bettje stepped briskly down the street. At the corner, she met Lisa and her family. "Where are the rest?" Lisa's father asked immediately.

Bettje hesitated. Too late, she realized that she had not thought things through. "They're at home," she faltered. "My father—I guess he's exhausted from his trip, and from fighting the sea."

Lisa's father said nothing. Did she detect a skeptical gleam in his eye? Bettje was not sure.

All morning she had to maintain the deception. "I guess Father's sick," she said lamely each time someone inquired after her family. Bettje wondered whether folks also noticed that Bernhard and Elizabeth were absent.

Fortunately, Lisa said nothing more about absences as she walked with Bettje after church. The two girls chattered gaily about other things.

On the doorstep at home, Bettje told herself, "Well, I had a good morning. Surely better than if I'd stayed at home."

Yet deep inside she sensed a hollowness, an emptiness that begged to be filled.

The weekdays, after all, were surprisingly normal. Father and Jan went about their business, working on the looms or on the dikes. There were times when Bettje felt like pinching herself to make sure

Meeting in a Barn   33

it had not all been a dream—a bad dream that would disappear if she waited long enough.

Then Sunday drew near again. Bettje's tension mounted. Could she face another Sunday filled with questions? Would people start acting hostile? Because in her heart of hearts, Bettje realized there was no hope that Father and Mother would come to church with her this Sunday either.

"We plan to attend a meeting at Uncle Leonhards'," Mother told Bettje on Saturday. "Obbe Phillips will be there. We greatly look forward to hearing him expound the Word of God. For months we've wanted to attend a meeting of the Leeuwarden brethren. We're so grateful that God is now giving us the courage to do it."

"But Mother," Bettje began miserably. Since the two of them were at the looms, away from the Claessen girls, she dared to express her feelings. "What if you get caught? What if they do to Father what they did to Andrew Claessen?"

Mother's eyes were like deep pools. "Bettje, how can I say it? We are casting ourselves upon the Lord's care. His will is precious to us—more precious than our lives. If suffering is part of God's will for us, then..." Suddenly Mother's voice failed, and the pools of her eyes overflowed. "I know, Bettje. It's hard. Very hard."

"I don't think I could face being orphaned like the Claessen girls," Bettje mumbled. Her own throat felt tight, too. Yet she didn't really want to cry.

Neither did Mother. Briskly she wiped her eyes. "We will leave the city before dawn tomorrow morning, and wait till after dark to return. It's possible no one will detect us."

Bettje protested in astonishment, "But how can you get through the gates?"

"There are other ways of leaving this city," Mother said mysteriously. "Carla and Lela have told us a thing or two. Those underground passageways where they lived for a while—they open out beyond the gate."

"You mean you'd be traveling in the sewers?" Bettje's voice squeaked with astonishment.

"Listen, Bettje," Mother said steadily. "We needn't call them sewers. They're underground passages, and Carla says it's possible to negotiate them without actually stepping in—in sewage."

"But still!" groaned Bettje. How humiliating! Before, she had basked in the knowledge that her father was a respected citizen, a dike reeve, and quite a wealthy man. Now what was he becoming? A fugitive who hid in the sewers! The thought was unbearable.

That Saturday night, Bettje's sleep was troubled. What was she going to do the next morning? She knew what her parents desired. And deep down she wanted to obey them. But what was a girl to do if forced to choose between obeying her parents and obeying the church?

In the end, it was her dread of facing folks' questions and stares that decided the matter for Bettje. Added to that was the sheer loneliness of knowing that the rest of the household would be leaving before dawn. She simply could not face it.

So when the others rose and took a cold breakfast of fruit and cheese, Bettje was with them. She stole with the rest to the bridge on Ormstrasse. She took one last breath of fresh air and plunged with the others into the putrid depths of the sewers.

Despite Mother's suggestion to not use the term, the fact remained that sewage ran along the trough of the passages. Yes, it was true that you could creep along a beam, if you bent nearly double. But if your foot should happen to slip, and you fell—!

Fortunately, nobody fell. And at length the family emerged from the vile tunnel, at an opening cunningly concealed behind a patch of bushes. Bettje drew in great breaths of fresh air, hoping to cleanse her lungs of those foul fumes.

Instead of traversing the top of the dike, the little group slunk along at the base, for now the sun was coming up and darkness no longer sheltered them. *We're like hunted animals*, Bettje thought sourly, glancing back to see whether anyone was on their trail.

At last they reached Uncle Leonhards'. "So many people!" whispered Bettje in amazement as they entered the upper barn, where piles of last year's hay lent a sweet aroma to the air.

Father smiled and whispered back, "The army of the Lord is growing."

The message that morning was unlike anything Bettje had ever heard. Obbe Phillips spoke about suffering—and how earnestly, how lovingly he spoke! The words were from Peter's epistles: *Beloved, think it not strange concerning the fiery trial which is to try you, as though some strange thing happened unto us: But rejoice, inasmuch as ye are partakers of Christ's sufferings; that, when his glory shall be revealed, ye may be glad also with exceeding joy.*

"Why should we be surprised if we are asked to suffer?" Obbe questioned. "Jesus suffered. Every day He suffered the hatred of people around Him. And if we are one with Him—what else can we expect? Then let us not be surprised, but instead rejoice, for the time will come when we can share also in His glory…"

Goose bumps rose along Bettje's spine. What Obbe said sounded so real, so immediate, so genuine. His words were impossible to disregard. Close her ears Bettje could not.

Afterwards there was a meal—simple food and heartfelt sharing. Bettje was amazed how included she felt, as though these people were old friends.

How could it be? All the way home, through the darkness and through the sewers, she puzzled over it. How could she feel almost tranquil, when the main thrust of Obbe's message had been to prepare people for future sufferings?

It simply made no sense.

Chapter Nine

A Walk With Lisa

"Run for the cellar! There's a visitor," Bettje whispered urgently. Like a flash the four Claessen girls disappeared. Heart pounding, Bettje opened the door. What could Lisa want, coming like this in the middle of the day?

Her friend greeted her warmly. "The weather was so nice, I just couldn't stay at home. So I thought I'd visit you."

Tumultuous feelings battled inside Bettje. Usually she was overjoyed to see Lisa. The two of them had always shared everything. But now…well, Bettje's life seemed to be turning upside down. Now there were more things than not that they could no longer share. What if she accidentally leaked something that endangered her family?

Flustered, Bettje mumbled a few words about the nice sunshine. "So you're staying a while?"

Lisa gave her a queer look. "Well, mayn't I?"

"Um, yes, of course. Have a seat on the bench."

But the moment Lisa had sat down, Bettje changed her mind. Why force the poor Claessen girls to stay down there throughout Lisa's visit? "Or we could go for a walk," she amended hastily.

Lisa hopped to her feet. "Let's! That's actually what I hoped you'd say."

What a peculiar sensation came over Bettje as she stepped freely out into the sunshine with her friend! Was she the same person who had scurried like a hunted rabbit through the sewers only a few days ago?

"I'd like to walk on the dikes," proposed Lisa.

Stifling her alarm, Bettje said, "What about the guards at the gate?"

Lisa sent her another queer look. "Why should we worry about them? We've done nothing wrong. Last I heard, this city wasn't preventing young girls from having a bit of fun."

"Well, no, of course not," Bettje said lamely. Yet her chest tightened as she approached the city gates with her unsuspecting friend. What if the guards had somehow found out about Sunday's clandestine excursion beneath the city walls?

The elderly guard's face was set in a habitual frown. "Name and address?"

"Ah, Peter, you know who we are," Lisa said saucily. "Just be a good fellow and let us through. All we want is to take a walk."

Somewhere in the recesses of Peter's scowl, a twinkle glimmered. "Go, then. How soon will you be back?"

"You'll know when you see us!" came Lisa's cheeky response.

Out of hearing distance from the guard, Bettje said laughingly, "You certainly have spunk."

Lisa tossed her head. "I've learned how to deal with those crusty guards. Most of them have a soft heart deep inside their red jerkins. Looking stern is part of their job, so that's what they do."

High on the dike, spring breezes fanned the girls' hair. Windmills flapped dutifully. Cows grazed serenely on emerald polders. All seemed light and freedom. Could this be the same world as the one of suspicion and danger where the Anabaptists chose to tread?

A jolt went through Bettje when, in that same moment, Lisa began speaking about Anabaptists. "I think it's scandalous the way those Anabaptists are trying to rule our country. Did you hear how they took the Amsterdam city hall a few weeks ago?"

Bettje's heart thudded against her chest. "In Amsterdam? Why, that is the most important city in the Netherlands!"

"I know. That's why I said it's scandalous. But it seems these followers of Melchior Hofmann do strange and foolish things. On May 11, a fellow by the name of Jan Matthys assembled an army of about fifty men and stormed the Amsterdam city hall! I guess he managed to take the authorities by surprise. But Jan didn't last long. Soon more soldiers came, and that was the end of Jan's foolhardy scheme. With things like that going on, I really can't blame the guards here in Leeuwarden for being extra suspicious—can you?"

"No, I guess not," Bettje faltered. If only Lisa would talk about something else! Hoping to change the subject, Bettje pointed to a horse and cart in the distance. "Just look at how high that man has piled his cart!"

But Lisa shrugged the comment aside and kept on talking about the Melchiorites. "They're so fanatical. They claim to have prophets, you know, who say that God's kingdom will soon be set up on earth. Over in Münster, Anabaptists have actually taken control of the city."

"I heard that. And the bishop's troops have placed Münster under siege," Bettje said, resigning herself to Lisa's topic. She would only arouse suspicion by being reluctant to talk about these things.

"Yet the funny thing is," Lisa went on, "their main leader—Hofmann himself—is in prison. And he had claimed that Strasburg will be the New Jerusalem! It's preposterous. We have one Anabaptist trying to take Strasburg, another claiming Münster, and a third attempting to grab Amsterdam! Don't you think Anabaptists are ridiculous?"

Bettje sighed inwardly. It seemed Lisa was determined to extract an opinion from her. If she were truthful she would have to admit, "I just don't know what to think." But Lisa wouldn't be content with such an answer. So Bettje said guardedly, "Not all Anabaptists are alike."

Lisa stared. "Now you're starting to defend them!"

"No, no," Bettje said miserably. How she wished this conversation had never started! No matter what she said, it turned out to be the wrong thing. "Couldn't we talk about something else for a change?" she pleaded.

"If you insist." Lisa sounded almost sullen—as though she resented Bettje's reluctance to discuss this burning issue. "I guess we might as well go home."

Striking up gay chatter was somehow impossible. As they trod along the dike, both girls tried to come up with small talk, but their efforts fell flat. Within Bettje a foreboding thought mushroomed: what if the whole purpose of Lisa's visit had been to scrutinize Bettje's feelings toward Anabaptists?

What if Lisa's family suspected something and were trying to check things out?

After all, they had every reason to be suspicious. The Weaver family had not been to church for two Sundays in a row.

Chapter Ten

Marpeck's Story

"I feel like I'm two different people," Bettje admitted when she stepped back into the house after bidding good-bye to Lisa.

Carla spoke up sympathetically. "I know the feeling. I once had a good friend... Her name was Reba."

Bettje felt like retorting, "I'm not yet speaking in the past tense about my friendship with Lisa!" But a stab of pain prevented her from saying anything. Was that what the future held? Was she destined to become a fugitive like Carla, bereft of all her former friends?

"What was it like out on the dike?" Anneken asked with a trace of envy.

"Oh, very nice. Just enough wind to set the windmills humming, but not enough to make big waves on the North Sea. At least I hope not. Of course I didn't actually see the sea."

Carla was still recalling memories of her former friend. "I could tell that Reba was awfully suspicious. Then suddenly, our friendship was over. She simply dropped out of sight."

"Didn't you mind?" Bettje asked.

An all-too-familiar look of pain curtained Carla's eyes. "Of course I minded," she said quietly.

Bettje apologized, "I'm sorry. I didn't mean to hurt you. It's just—there are so many things—I mean…" Her voice trailed off. What was the use in trying to put into words the perplexity of her life?

What was the use, indeed? But for a young, bewildered person, putting things into words can be needful. Bettje tossed and turned that night, unable to sleep. Staring her in the face was the awful specter of their whole neighborhood turning against them, perhaps even driving them away.

"Yet how could they do it?" Bettje kept asking herself, there in the darkness of her bedroom. "Everybody likes Father. Why, the Water Authorities could hardly wait till he got home from his trip! Surely they wouldn't turn against such an important person…"

But then she recalled the hatred lurking in Lisa's voice whenever she spoke about Anabaptists. Such hatred knew no bounds, cared nothing for long-blossoming friendships…

Suddenly Bettje realized that her parents were still in the kitchen. "I simply must talk with someone," she told herself as she dressed and stole down the hall.

Father and Mother sat near the hearth. A few remaining embers in the fireplace cast an eerie glow on their faces. They did not seem surprised when Bettje appeared.

"Are you having trouble falling asleep?" Mother asked kindly. She pulled another chair closer. "Sit here if you like."

Awkwardly, Bettje took the chair. "Maybe it's just my imagination, but it seemed to me that Lisa was after something today. Like—like she meant to spy on our family."

Neither of her parents spoke immediately. Eventually Father cleared his throat. "Such things are quite possible."

"But if that's the case, then Lisa isn't a true friend anymore!" Bettje wailed.

Slowly, Father told her, "Jesus said, 'Ye shall be hated of all men for my sake.' And He also said, 'If the world hate you, ye know that it hated me before it hated you.'"

Bettje's hands twisted tightly in her lap. "I wish it wouldn't have to be like that."

"I understand," Mother said softly.

"And once folks do find out—what then? Will they—?" Bettje broke off. The horror of Andrew Claessen's death still haunted her.

"We don't know what they will do. But on Sunday we heard what glorious rejoicing we may expect if we suffer for Jesus' sake." Father's voice was steady.

Almost pleadingly, Bettje asked, "Isn't there a chance that—that they would be kind to you, Father? I mean, because of all you have done for the city. How could they turn against you?"

Father's eyes took on a faraway look. "You make me think of a man I learned to know during my trip. His name is Pilgram Marpeck. He was born in an Austrian province to wealthy parents, and received an education as an engineer. As a young man he became a member of his city's council, besides being a skillful mining engineer. Pilgram was definitely what you would call a respected citizen.

"But the Lord was also working on Pilgram's heart. Born a Catholic, he watched the reform movements with interest. Yet he saw that the results were disappointing. State church members showed little true zeal for God. Eventually Pilgram fixed his eyes on the truth and was baptized by the brethren upon confession of his faith.

"Skillful mining engineer or not, Marpeck had to flee from his city. Anabaptists weren't allowed there. With his wife and children he moved to Alsace, and eventually settled in Strasburg."

Father leaned back thoughtfully. "I found Strasburg an interesting town. I don't think there's another city in all Europe where Anabaptists are so well tolerated."

"You mean they are allowed to openly practice their faith?" Mother questioned.

"Well...not exactly. The State Church there is Zwingli's. The Strasburg authorities have published numerous mandates against the brethren, banishing them from the city. Those who are banished and later return are threatened with torture... Yet when I was there, somebody said Strasburg has some 2000 Anabaptists."

"Isn't Strasburg where Melchior Hofmann is imprisoned?" Mother asked.

"Yes, and he has deluded many people into believing that Strasburg will be the New Jerusalem, headquarters of God's kingdom on earth." Father shook his head. "Oh, how sad, that some have such a warped view of God's plan! According to the Bible, God's kingdom is in our hearts. Right here and now, if we believe in Christ's saving blood.

"But getting back to Pilgram Marpeck—in Strasburg his skill as an engineer was soon recognized. He designed an aqueduct to bring water into the city, and supervised its construction. Not only that, but Pilgram has a knowledge of rafting. Strasburg owns timber lands in the Black Forest; under Marpeck's direction, the logs are rafted down the Rhine to the city.

"Inevitably, the authorities found out that Pilgram is one of the brethren—a minister, in fact. At first they were quite lenient with him. The city council disputed with him, trying to make him recant. But Pilgram clung to the truth, so a few years ago he was banished from Strasburg. The only leniency shown him was that they allowed him a few weeks to dispose of his property before he left. So...even a man as gifted as Marpeck was not tolerated by the authorities."

Mother asked, "Obbe Phillips is a surgeon, is he not?"

"Yes. He has helped many ailing people," Father agreed. "So far, Obbe has not been banished from Leeuwarden."

Bettje stared thoughtfully at the dying embers. "Getting banished... at least it would not be as bad as...as..." It seemed she could never utter those horrible words.

"God is merciful," Father said. "Whatever He allows, we want to submit to it."

Bettje got slowly to her feet. "I feel better now."

"Jesus gives us true peace, no matter what," Mother assured her warmly.

Chapter Eleven

Discovered!

Rain spat from lowering clouds as a group of thirteen people emerged from the sewer opening below the dike. Even though the dike's tall structure provided some shelter, Bettje was thoroughly soaked by the time she entered Uncle Leonhard's barn.

Today was special. At least that was what Mother had said, her eyes shining as she broke the news to Bettje. Five people were to receive baptism today: Father, Mother, Bernhard, Elizabeth and Carla.

Bettje could easily see that her parents and Carla were very happy about it. For them, this really was a special day. But inside Bettje clamored a voice that reminded her: now her parents would be truly "Anabaptist"—twice-baptized. Now there would be no turning back. No hope remained of ever again leading a normal life. Her family would be branded with a label of hatred.

Sometimes Bettje ached all over with the desire to just be normal again. If only she had appreciated her life more, back in the days when it still flowed easily and sweetly! But she had taken it all for granted. And now it was gone forever.

Yet despite the glum feelings, Bettje found herself once again caught up by Obbe's message, carried along like a ship on a strong sea current. He told of the day when Jesus sought baptism from John. "Here we have the greatest testimony to the importance of baptism," Obbe declared. "The Son of God Himself desired baptism, and said for our benefit, 'Thus it becometh us to fulfill all righteousness.'"

It seemed that Obbe could never praise Jesus enough. "Notice the three titles John the Baptist gave to Jesus here at the Jordan! They are titles of power, titles that bless His followers. John called Jesus the 'Lamb of God'—our redeemer! He also called Him the 'Son of God'—worthy of all our adoration. And then he called Him the 'one who baptizes with the Holy Ghost.' Yes, Jesus is our brother; and as we believe and are baptized, He imparts His very life to us in the form of the Spirit."

The words were so powerful—yet the ceremony itself so simple. Just an outpouring of water, a laying on of hands, and a raising up to newness of life. That was all it took to guarantee the world's hatred for the rest of the person's life.

Among the brethren who had met today were two other girls close to Carla's and Bettje's age. Their names were Hannah and Gertrude. Today, somehow, Bettje felt awkward with this group of girls. The other three were baptized, she knew; whereas she—who was she? Certainly not one who even sought baptism. She was just a girl who came here because there was really no alternative, unless she wished to stay at home alone.

Sadly she thought, *I don't have any real friends anymore. Wherever I go, I'm a misfit. I just know things will never be the same again between Lisa and me.*

To Bettje's surprise—and consternation—four days later, Lisa came again to visit. Bettje waited as long as she dared to open the door, thus giving the Claessen girls plenty of time to flee into the cellar.

"Good morning, Lisa," Bettje said, very politely.

Lisa's smile was so wide that it seemed put-on. "Good morning, yourself! Why do you sound so formal, as though I were an official at your door?" she bantered.

Bettje replied, "I'm sorry if I sounded formal"—but even that came out stiffly. Inwardly she was thinking, *I'm not going for a walk with Lisa this time. We'll stay right here in the kitchen with Mother.*

So when Lisa suggested, "Shall we take another walk along the dikes?" Bettje shook her head. "Sorry, I don't feel like it this morning."

Lisa gave her a narrow look. "Are you sick, or what?"

Again Bettje shook her head. "Not sick. Just not feeling up to it. You can have a seat there. So what have you been doing these days?"

"Oh, just the usual," Lisa sighed. "Carding and spinning wool. I get sick and tired of it."

"Weavers certainly appreciate all the carding and spinning you do," Bettje reminded her.

"Well, I didn't come here to talk about spinning. I came here to get away from it," Lisa pouted.

Uh-oh, thought Bettje, *this conversation is not going very well.* It made her ache inwardly, for so it had never been in the old days. Lisa and she could always talk easily and freely.

Mother did her part to aid the floundering conversation, asking pleasant questions about Lisa's family. But eventually Lisa asked, "Can I see your looms, Bettje? I always like to see the fabrics you make."

Such a proposition—from a girl who claimed to be sick of spinning—was blatantly false. Lisa had never before displayed such an interest in weaving. To Bettje it was as plain as day that Lisa was contriving to be alone with her.

It was the last thing Bettje wanted. What of the poor Claessen girls, ensconced down below in the cellar?

But what could she do? Pretend that she didn't feel up to it, as she had when Lisa proposed a walk? That wouldn't work.

A pleading glance in Mother's direction brought no aid. Apparently Mother felt just as helpless as Bettje toward this girl who, whether she knew it or not, was acting like a busybody.

"All right," conceded Bettje, leading the way to the back.

"The way you act, I could think you're hiding something back here," Lisa said.

"Oh, you're quite welcome to inspect our looms. We have three now, since I've learned to weave as well," responded Bettje, trying to hide her alarm beneath nonchalance. Quickly she took her seat at a loom and sent the shuttle flying. If any accidental sounds came up from the cellar, she could at least mask them with some noise of her own. Besides, maybe Lisa wouldn't ask so many questions if she pretended to be busy.

But that was a vain hope. Lisa drew close, her brow puckered into a frown. "Bettje, I've a question I simply must ask. Somebody told us your parents have been rebaptized. Tell me it isn't true!"

The urgency in her voice touched Bettje. Her friend really did care. But what, oh what, should she say?

"Don't be afraid to tell me," Lisa coaxed. "I'm your friend. I would never, never betray you."

The words were warm enough. Yet something in the tone did not ring true. Finally Bettje asked, "Who was saying things like that to you?"

Like the closing of a door, a sullen look covered Lisa's face. "I can't tell you that."

"Maybe I also have things I cannot tell you," Bettje said, hating the coldness in her voice. Something inside her screamed, "No, it can't be true that my best friend and I are talking like this to each other!" Yet she forced herself to continue. "If what you said were true, Lisa, do you think I'd want to talk about it? And if it's not true—well, then, there's nothing to talk about, is there?"

Now there was anger in Lisa's eyes. "It must be true, then, or else you would deny it! Your parents are Anabaptists! Oh, Bettje!"

Lisa got up and flung herself out the back door. Her last words seemed to echo in the room. "Your parents are Anabaptists. Oh, Bettje!"

The note of wild despair matched precisely the desolation in Bettje's heart.

Chapter Twelve

The Emperor's Decree

See Martyrs Mirror pages 442, 443

Down from the city hall floated the high, shrill notes of a bugle. Bettje's shuttle halted abruptly. She looked across at Mother, who was busy at the other loom.

"Somebody must be giving an announcement at the city hall." There was a tremor in Mother's voice.

"Will we go?" asked Bettje. At the summons of a bugle, every citizen was expected to drop what he was doing and head for the town square. The bugling meant that the bishop—or the queen—or even the emperor—was publishing a decree, and people were supposed to pay attention.

"Well," said Mother, "the law says that at least one person from each household is to go. Since Father and Jan are working on the dikes, they will probably not even hear the summons, let alone show up for the broadcast."

"So that means you should go. I'll go with you," Bettje said, though not really understanding why she offered that. Those royal decrees were rarely about anything pleasant. What morbid attraction made her want to hear it for herself?

"Let's see whether the girls agree to stay alone while we're gone," Mother suggested.

Leaving her loom, Bettje followed Mother to the kitchen. Carla said immediately, "We heard the bugle."

"Would you be all right here by yourselves if we both go?" asked Mother.

"Of course." Carla looked at her sisters, who all nodded.

It was June 10, 1535, and as Bettje stepped into the street with her mother she couldn't help thinking this might be a day she would never forget. What life-changing—or even life-threatening—decree awaited them up there at the city hall?

Throngs of people were gathering in the square. High on the steps of the city hall stood the royal emissary, his blue robe billowing in the wind. When the square was filled from end to end with people, the bugles sounded again to signal the start of the announcement.

Pompously the herald unrolled his paper and began to read. The words were from the Emperor Charles himself. First came an entire paragraph saying to whom the decree was being sent: a long list of important sounding titles such as chancellors, presidents, councilors, bailiffs, judges, governors; and then at the end of the paragraph was included "and their subjects."

So that means me too, thought Bettje.

Now came the words that sent shivers up and down her spine. "In order to guard against the errors which many sectarians have dared for some time to sow in our territories, against our holy Christian faith…"

This was a decree against the Anabaptists! The realization hit Bettje like a blow.

Next followed some long, jumbled sentences filled with words like decrees, statutes, transgressors, punished, false doctrine, seduce. As far as Bettje could gather, the emperor was complaining that earlier decrees against the Anabaptists had not been effective, so he was taking stronger measures.

"Cause it to be proclaimed within every place of your dominion, that all of those polluted by the accursed sect of the Anabaptists... shall incur the loss of life and property, and be brought to the most extreme punishment, without delay. All who have been rebaptized, or who secretly have harbored Anabaptists, shall be executed with the sword...

"We expressly command all subjects to report any Anabaptists to the officers... If anyone shall know of such persons, and not report them, he shall be punished...

"But he who shall report them shall have one third of their confiscated property...

"Because of their evil doctrine, we will not permit that any Anabaptists shall have any mercy shown them, but that they shall be punished without delay...

"And in order to do this...we give each and all of you full power and special command.

"Subscribed by the Emperor and his council, and signed."

A hush fell over the square, as though a wind from the North Pole had frozen the crowd into statues of horror.

Few people could turn away scot-free from those harsh commands. Few in Leeuwarden were not acquainted with an Anabaptist, whether Obbenite or Melchiorite. And who knew how many were actually sympathizers, or even one of the brethren themselves?

Mother did not move, so Bettje stayed still as well. Then, hearing a familiar voice at her elbow, she whirled. "Father! Jan!" she choked out.

"We thought you were out on the dikes," Mother said, her voice a mixture of questions and gladness.

"We hurried back because someone told us there is to be a proclamation. Shall we go home now?" Father suggested.

Home. The word had a hollow ring. How much longer would that be home?

Questions filling her mind, Bettje turned to Father as they hurried down the street. "Does that proclamation mean we have to move out of the country?"

Father smiled kindly. "Let's wait to talk till we're home."

Once there, he quickly explained to the Claessen girls, "The emperor has published a decree against all Anabaptists. Anyone who knows of them is to report them. Anabaptists who are caught will be punished without delay."

Bettje watched as her friends' faces turned pale. "What are we going to do?" asked Lela.

"A meeting is being held tonight at Bernhards' home," Father replied. "Will you girls be all right here with Jan for company while Mother and I are gone?"

Bettje glanced at Carla, who nodded bravely. Not waiting to eat supper, Father and Mother hurried away. How slowly the next two hours passed for Bettje! Fear stalked the dark windows and whispered at the door. Any moment, some zealous Anabaptist-hunters could break into the Weaver home. By this time a lot of people in Leeuwarden knew that the Weavers were not attending church.

The door latch rattled. Bettje started up, her heart racing. Relief washed over her as Father and Mother appeared. What was that look on their faces? Excitement? Apprehension?

Without waiting for any questions, Father began, "Seven families have decided to leave the Netherlands. Long ago, Jesus advised His followers to flee the oppression in Judea, and now we will do the same. In so doing we will carry His truth to other lands and cause the church to grow."

"But where can we go? Most of Europe is under Charles the

emperor. How can we escape his decree?" Jan asked despairingly.

"I know of a place where we can hope to live in peace," Father replied mysteriously. "However, I won't tell you right now where we're going. That way, if people ask questions, you can say you don't know."

Now it was Mother's turn to speak. "Obbe Phillips thought our group should have a leader. So the brethren cast votes, and Father has been ordained a minister."

Bettje stared in disbelief. Her father—an Anabaptist minister! Jan, too, looked stunned.

Choosing not to say anything about his new calling, Father said practically, "By tomorrow night we should be on the move. We can take only what we can carry. So I imagine you women will need to think about that. But first, let's get some sleep."

Sleep? Did Father expect to sleep? Inside the space of half a day, the Weaver family had become fugitives because of the emperor's decree, they had made plans to flee the country, and Father had become a minister for a group of heretics.

Even if Father thought he would sleep, Bettje felt sure she wouldn't.

Chapter Thirteen

On the Move

All night they walked, laden with bundles. The adults took turns carrying Mary, who was very brave and never cried. As they stole through the darkness, others joined them. Bernhard and Elizabeth were part of the group, and so were Uncle Leonhards with their two married sons and their families.

Never had a night seemed so long. Bettje's feet became leaden with weariness, and her eyelids threatened to droop even while she walked. But at last, at last, a thin line of dawn-light showed on the eastern horizon.

"Will we walk all day too?" Anneken asked plaintively.

"No. We will lie down and sleep," Father promised.

"In a house?" came Anneken's eager question.

Mother answered, "No, Anneken. Perhaps in the woods."

"You mean nobody would want to give us shelter?" Bettje wondered.

Mother cleared her throat. "Some might. There are many kind-hearted people. But Bettje, think about it. Even if someone offered to take us in, would we want to endanger those people by accepting the offer?"

Words from the decree trickled like icy water through Bettje's mind: "All who have secretly harbored Anabaptists shall be executed with the sword."

The whole world had turned against them. What a horrible thought! What use was there in fleeing? Where in all the lands of the terrible Emperor Charles did Father expect to find a haven?

In a thick copse of trees they took shelter for the day, hoping that no nearby farmers would discover them. After a meager meal, Bettje lay on her blanket trying to get comfortable on the ground. Oh, for her soft bed at home! Who would sleep in that bed now? Who would greedily claim their home, not caring that the former occupants had become fugitives?

To her surprise, Bettje actually slept for a while. Suddenly she awoke to the sound of a voice asking gruffly, "What is going on here?"

There stood a Dutch farmer in rough pantaloons and a floppy cap. His blue eyes ranged in astonishment over the motley group lying under the trees.

Before anyone could answer his question, the stranger began, "Are you—?" Then he stopped, raising a hand. "Don't answer! I don't want to know who you are! I heard the emperor's decree. I have seen nothing. I know nothing." With that, he stamped away in his wooden clogs.

Momentarily he stopped and flung back over his shoulder, "I hope you understand. I hate that emperor as much as you do, and would never treat you like this, if—if…" Then he no longer knew what to say. Staring after his retreating back, Bettje thought she saw him wipe his eyes.

When night came, the march resumed. Bettje muttered to her brother, "We must be heading for the sea."

On the Move

"Of course. That's pretty obvious." He sounded scornful, as though he'd expected her to realize that long ago.

"Apparently we'll take ship on the North Sea, then. But where to? England?"

"I don't know," Jan admitted. "I rather wish Father would tell us. But his idea is that if someone questions us, it's better if we know very little."

Just then a thought struck Bettje—a thought so startling that it stopped her in her tracks. "Do you think we might even cross the Atlantic, to that new land discovered by Columbus and Cartier?"

"I've thought of that." Through the darkness, Bettje detected a note of excitement in her brother's voice. "But I doubt it. Imagine taking this many women and children across the ocean—to a land inhabited by savages? We might as well let the authorities here in the Netherlands get rid of us in their own way."

Now his voice held bitterness, and it found an echo in Bettje's heart. Was there any pain like the pain of being turned out of one's home by people who once had been friends?

Later, trudging along beside Carla, Bettje mused, "I wonder how Lisa feels by this time. No doubt she's noticed that we're gone."

"I think she might be sad. Was she not a true friend?" Carla queried.

"At one time she was. But during her last visit...it seemed she had turned against us. Her main reason for coming was to spy on us."

"Maybe you imagined that," Carla objected.

"I don't think so. Didn't you say your friend Reba also turned against you?" demanded Bettje.

"Well, yes," came Carla's lame reply.

Gray dawn was creeping up from the east when Bettje became aware of a new sound: the rhythmic slap-slap-slap of waves against a shore.

"I hear the sea, Lela," she exclaimed.

Ahead, dark shapes of buildings loomed against the sky. "A town," whispered Carla. "Your father is leading us straight toward it."

"Must be a seaport," Bettje whispered.

Father directed them now to a rough trail bypassing the buildings. There were the gray waters of the North Sea, stretching away to the horizon. Wave after wave rolled in over the sandy beach.

Father's eyes searched the sea and the shore. "No ship," he said, sounding puzzled.

"So you expected one to be here?" Jan asked, seizing the chance to find out his plans.

"A wool merchant I know—one of the Hanseatic League—was going to anchor his ship here for several months. Perhaps he hasn't arrived yet. I'm going to make some inquiries. Try to stay out of sight behind these buildings."

Bettje watched her father stride toward another building. What if he was caught? What if she never saw him again?

But he was back soon, even wearing a smile. "A man told me that the merchant decided to move on to the next seaport, northward up the coast. We're to find him there."

"More walking," groaned Bettje, too quietly for Father to hear.

"He also said—" and now Father's smile widened— "that he's not saying we may sleep in his warehouses. At the same time, neither is he saying that we may not."

Bernhard spoke up. "We would be endangering him if we did."

"I know. I told him we would take shelter in those woods over there."

"Good thing it's summer," Bettje said to Carla as they spread their blankets beneath the trees.

"Did you know," began Carla, "that when Jesus advised His followers to flee from Judea, He said, 'Pray that your flight be not in the winter'? Jesus cares about details like that."

Lying there on the ground, Bettje pondered her friend's words. Carla seemed to think Jesus really cared about what happened to His people. Was it true? Did He care that she was lying homeless in a forest?

Chapter Fourteen

Setting Sail

Boarding a ship for the very first time was exciting, even for fugitives. The *Journeyman* rode high on the water, sails flapping idly from three towering masts. Bettje's heart beat fast as she walked the gangplank onto the ship's deck. How strange it was to feel the deck heaving beneath her feet! Leaning over the rail, Bettje stared at the green waves nudging the ship's wooden sides.

The ship still rode at anchor. Porters were busily loading huge bales of wool and woven goods. "We must be going someplace in Europe, and not to America," Bettje whispered to Jan. "Savages don't need tons of wool and fabric, do they?"

That made her brother smile. "You know what I hope? Maybe once we're actually underway, Father will finally tell us where we're going. In the meantime, I want to watch the crew hoist the sails!"

To his disappointment, however, all passengers were ordered below decks. "I suppose the sailors think we'd just get in their way," Jan mumbled, descending the ladder ahead of Bettje.

From the depths of the hold rose a dank, unpleasant odor. "Not quite as bad as the sewers," Bettje commented to Carla.

A single lantern swayed from a beam. The compartment was small, its walls lined with bunks, two above each other. "I thought maybe we'd have to find room among the bales of wool," said Lela, ever the one to find humor in a situation.

Once the entire group of fugitives had descended the ladder, the compartment was quite crowded. Bettje turned expectantly to Father. When was he going to tell them?

But still he remained silent. Soon shouts rang up on the deck as the sails were hoisted and the anchors pulled in. Suddenly the ship's movement changed. Though it still heaved with the waves, now there was also a steady forward thrust.

"We've started off!" Bettje whispered to Hannah. "But I surely wish I knew where we're going."

At last Father stood up, clearing his throat. "I guess some of you are still wondering where we're going. This is a ship of the Hanseatic League—the organization that controls many seaports along the Baltic Coast. In my travels I've been to many of those seaports—even as far as Gdansk, on the Vistula River in Poland. And that's where we're going: Poland."

"We can't speak Polish," blurted out Titus Claessen.

Father smiled. "No, but most of us understand some German. The area where we're going is mostly held by descendants of German knights who settled there in the past few centuries."

"And you already know that we'll be welcome in Poland?" questioned Jan.

"Yes. In fact, I have a personal invitation from a nobleman who owns much land in the Vistula River delta. His land is very fertile—but also marshy. Now can you guess why this nobleman might welcome tenants from the Netherlands?"

Jan was beaming. "I certainly can! He needs folks who know a thing or two about drainage!" His voice held a note of anticipation, as though he already looked forward to ditch-digging.

"Right. Count Frankfurt has a large dairy and many cows. But

Setting Sail   61

right now, even though he owns hundreds of acres of land, he can barely raise enough crops to feed his cows. So our challenge will be…" Father paused, smiling. "I guess our challenge will be to 'make the dry land appear.'"

Father sat down on his bunk. The men were soon engrossed in a discussion about draining marshes. Bettje commented to Hannah, "Listening to them talk, you'd think they can hardly wait to start shoveling mud!"

"It's nice that they look forward to the work they'll be doing," her friend responded.

Lela wondered, "Do you think the sailors would let us go up on the deck now? I'd so like to see the sails when they're full of wind."

"I'll ask," offered Titus. Up the ladder he clambered. A grin covered his face when he returned. "They said we can come up, though not more than ten at a time. And we have to stay on the aft deck so we're out of the sailors' way."

When her turn came, Bettje started up the ladder. It swung wildly as the ship pitched with the waves. Twice she nearly lost her footing and fell. "That was scary!" she gasped as she scrambled out onto the deck.

But the view was worth the scare. Eastward across the scudding waves lay the long, low profile of the Netherlands. "Maybe this is the last time we'll see our homeland," Bettje whispered to Carla.

"Perhaps," she agreed. "For myself, I'm glad to leave Holland behind. Every mile across the waves takes us farther away from the Emperor Charles."

Hannah pointed out glumly, "No doubt the Vistula delta is also a part of Charles's empire."

"Actually, no, Poland is not part of the empire," Carla told her. "So if those German noblemen invited us to come, they won't let the emperor harm us with his decrees."

Anneken was peering high up into the rigging, where the sails billowed taut and full. "It feels like we're flying, and the sails are our wings!" she cried.

The deck swooped and dived beneath their feet. *Maybe Anneken is right*, thought Bettje. *Maybe this is how it feels to fly.*

Then suddenly, she was sick. And soon every one of the girls was sick as well. "My—my stomach doesn't like flying," Bettje gasped in a lame attempt at humor.

Carla moaned, "Let's go and lie down."

"But I don't know if I can manage that ladder," Carla said miserably.

Somehow they all staggered down the treacherously tossing ladder. Even though the bunks were hard and rough, never had a bed seemed more welcome to poor Bettje!

Without exception, every last passenger grew seasick as the ship labored onward. Loathsome odors and wretched moans filled the small compartment.

Whenever she was not too sick to think, Bettje found herself longing for the wide green polders of home, and for the blessed sensation of solid ground beneath her feet. Oh, why had she agreed to leave with her parents? She could have stayed safe in Holland, living with Lisa's family. Surely they would have accepted her. She was not a heretic like the others.

But there was no way she could escape this horrible ship now. As night drew on, the moans seemed to grow more pitiful. The worst part of it was, not even the mothers could hold up their heads long enough to help anyone else.

"Couldn't the ship stop on land till we feel better?" Bettje groaned.

Father's answer was barely above a whisper. "Docking a ship isn't easy. Besides, I don't know if there's a port nearby."

Down the hatch came a harsh command: "Lights out for the night!"

Somehow, Bernhard managed to lift one arm to extinguish the lantern. Darkness smothered the hold like a thick black blanket. Yet still the moans continued. Would no one be able to sleep?

Setting Sail

Chapter Fifteen

On the Shoals

A rending, grinding crash tore through Bettje's sickly stupor. In the darkness she heard others shifting in their bunks, asking bewildered questions. "What happened?" "What was that?"

Adam Claessen's voice rose shrilly above the rest. "Are we having a shipwreck?"

As if in response to his cry, the entire ship shuddered, then lurched to a halt. Heedless of her stomach, Bettje sat up, staring wildly into the thick darkness. Any moment these rough planks beside her bunk might buckle, and the sea would pour in over the helpless little group entrapped in the hold.

Then, to her right, she heard Bernhard's calm voice. He was praying. Though Bettje had heard Father praying numerous times since he'd turned Anabaptist, these "heretic" prayers never failed to astound her. They were so real, as if God was right here, transforming this odorous place into a lofty cathedral.

"Lord, we trust in Your power. You can save our earthly lives if that is Your will. You have power over the waves and the sea. But if our bodies are to perish now, may You guard each soul in Your care, that peradventure none may perish eternally," Bernhard prayed.

That last part brought uneasiness to Bettje. What did he mean by perishing eternally? Wasn't that what happened to anyone who was untrue to the holy mother church? Faced with a sinister death beneath the waves, did Bernhard suddenly regret having turned away from the church?

"Lord, we thank You for guiding us into all truth. Be with us now and forever," Bernhard prayed on.

Bettje shook her head in bewilderment. That didn't sound like a man suffering from regret!

Shouts and thuds filtered down from the deck. With a thump, the hatch was wrenched open and a voice shouted, "We've run aground! All hands needed for bailing!"

"We must have hit a sandbar and sprung a leak." That was Father's voice. "These shoals among the Friesian Islands have caught many a ship. I think I could get up and help with the bailing."

He sounded surprisingly strong, considering how sick he had appeared before the light was extinguished. Suddenly Bettje realized that she, too, felt better. "And no wonder," she whispered to herself. "Now that we're stuck on a sandbar that awful rolling sensation has stopped."

An ironic chuckle escaped her lips. She had wished desperately that the ship would stop—and her wish had come true. Much good it would do, though, if the ship broke up and sent them all to a watery grave.

For some minutes the ship still groaned and shifted, as though trying in vain to free itself from the sandbar. Then the *Journeyman* lay still and resigned. Bettje knew very little about sailing, but she could guess that the crew must have been working frantically to bring down the sails, knowing that the ship would only destroy itself as long as the wind had a hold on it.

Bettje heard groping noises as several men found the ladder and began climbing. Then a new sound sent a chill through her. Water was sloshing in the bottom of the hold!

Bettje began to sob. To her left, Anneken and Mary were also crying.

Then a hand touched Bettje's shoulder, and Mother's voice sounded close by. "Don't be afraid, Bettje. God is with us."

In amazement, Bettje dashed away her tears. How had Mother, sick as she was, managed to reach her bunk? "Aren't you sick anymore?" Bettje mumbled.

"I feel better, now that the ship's rolling has stopped. Don't you?" asked Mother, sitting on the side of Bettje's bunk.

Bettje sniffed back a sob. "Maybe my stomach feels better. But it's horrible to think that we—that we might all drown."

Mother's hand tightened on her shoulder. "God is in control. His will is all that matters."

Bettje refused to be comforted. "We might as well have stayed in the Netherlands. That would have been better than being swallowed by the ocean."

Cheerfully, Mother pointed out, "The ship doesn't seem to be sinking. We might soon break free and continue our journey."

Still glum, Bettje muttered, "But then we'll just get sick again."

Mother laughed softly. "It seems you are determined to be unhappy, Bettje."

That hurt. How could Mother laugh when they were all in such desperate straits?

Mother moved on. Now Bettje heard her saying, "There, there, Mary. God is taking care of us."

Bettje could make no sense out of the confused jumble of sounds coming from overhead. Shouts, splashes and thumps mingled into one terrifying cacophony. If only morning would come! Then at least the men would be able to see what they were doing.

A sudden hope gripped Bettje. What if, when dawn broke, they would see land not far away? Perhaps they could all escape from the ship in lifeboats before its battered hulk sank!

High up on the compartment wall, Bettje had noticed some cracks where light had filtered in yesterday. Now she kept her eyes trained on the spot where she thought the cracks had been. When, oh when, would daylight come?

Or had the *Journeyman* already sunk so far that those cracks were now submerged beneath the water?

Chapter Sixteen

Freed

Wearily, Father staggered down the ladder. Collapsing onto the bunk, he reported, "We should be okay. We're able to bail fast enough that the ship won't sink."

"That's good," said Mother. "So the damage is not too serious?"

Father shook his head. "It could be a lot worse, anyway. Captain Nordstrom is still hoping we can float free and continue on—or at least make it to the nearest port for repairs. A strong wind blowing from the southeast is all it would take to free this ship, providing the crew hoists the right amount of sails."

"Is the wind from the northwest right now?" wondered Samuel, the middle Claessen boy.

"I think so. And do you know what? Before I came below, Captain Nordstrom asked us to pray for a change of wind."

"That's interesting," remarked Uncle Leonhard. "Why doesn't the captain himself pray?"

Father smiled. "Maybe he does. But he seemed to think our prayers would be more effective than his."

"He must not be very strongly against the brethren," Mother said.

"No, he is not. He and I have been friends for many years. Because of the emperor's decree, I was very hesitant about asking him to take us on this voyage. But Abel was more than willing. That's the captain's first name, by the way—Abel."

"Perhaps God will bless him for having compassion on us," suggested Elizabeth.

Father heaved himself from the bunk and knelt on the soggy floorboards. "Let's pray now."

Kneeling along with the rest, Bettje listened as the brethren poured out their hearts to God. They thanked Him for His loving care and asked for His protection. Though they also asked that the wind might change, the request was followed by submission to God's will.

All that day and the next night, the *Journeyman* remained fast on the sandbar. Hour after hour the men and boys took turns bailing.

When morning came again, Bettje saw to her horror that the water in the hold was now several inches deep. Would death for them all come an inch at a time as the relentless sea won the battle?

Then from the deck sounded shouts of gladness, followed by the rattle and creak of rigging. "They're hoisting sails!" Father exclaimed. "The wind must have changed."

How the ship groaned as the southeast wind caught the sails! A mighty tussle was on between the wind and the sandbar. Both were trying to claim the *Journeyman*!

Finally, with one last convulsive groan, and a terrific grinding of wood on sand, the ship floated free.

"I never thought I could be so glad for the feel of waves beneath us again," chuckled the irrepressible Lela.

The bailing continued at a furious pace, for now the water poured even faster through the leak. Up, up came the water, until it reached halfway to Bettje's knees. Fearfully she asked, "Is it far to the next port?"

"No. Abel says it is not far at all," Father answered reassuringly.

Freed

"We can make it. Abel asked us to keep on praying."

Automatically, Bettje touched the prayer beads she always wore around her neck. But somehow she could not bring herself to repeat any prayers to the Mother Mary. Instead she listened to the heartfelt prayers of the men.

Jan's excited voice echoed down the hatch. "We can see land! Would you like to come up and see it, Bettje?"

Weakly she lifted her head, then laid it down again. "I'm too sick," she moaned. Those waves, though ever so welcome as they bore the ship to land, were making some of the passengers sick again.

Bettje dozed fitfully. Sometime later she awoke to Carla's touch. "Have you noticed? We're at anchor," her friend said happily.

"Oooh. Feels good," mumbled Bettje. "I hope I'll be well enough to climb that ladder."

Father spoke up. "We can't leave the ship just yet. Abel has gone ashore to make arrangements. This is just a tiny port near a village of northern Friesland. I think we have created quite a stir among the villagers. A ship this size rarely docks here!"

"How did the captain know that the harbor would be deep enough for the *Journeyman*?" wondered Bernhard.

Father admitted, "He knew he was taking a chance. But staying on the sea in such a battered condition would have been an even greater risk."

"I have wondered," began Leonhard, "whether we should keep quiet about our faith? I mean, while we seek lodging in the village while the ship is being repaired."

There was a short silence. Then Father asked slowly, "I suppose you are thinking of the risk people take if they offer shelter to the brethren?"

"That was my thought, yes," responded Leonhard.

After a short discussion, the men agreed to Leonhard's suggestion. Leonhard's concluding remark was, "We don't want to needlessly endanger anyone."

Bettje studied her father's face in the lantern light. He seemed troubled. Didn't he agree with Leonhard's plan? To herself Bettje said, "I'm surely glad Leonhard suggested that. We'll be safer if people don't know why we're fleeing from the Netherlands."

Later on that day the men went ashore to seek lodging. Since she felt better again, Bettje went up on deck with her friends. Pointing delightedly toward shore, she exclaimed, "Cows! Over there are some real cows in a real field."

"Oh, Bettje, you sound like you haven't seen a farm for months," Carla said with a chuckle.

"It feels like months," Bettje grumbled. "When you're that sick, a single minute feels like a whole day."

The village was indeed small, and so was the harbor. The *Journeyman* had anchored well away from shore. Rising and dipping with the swells, the rowboat with Father and the other men labored toward land.

"Let's stay up here till the men come back," suggested Hannah. "It feels so good to breathe pure, fresh air."

So the girls leaned against the railing and watched while the men, mere specks in the distance, walked up to the village. Soon, though, Bettje felt faint. "I wonder if it's okay to lie down here on deck?" she faltered.

Carla whirled to look at her. "Are you sick? Here, lie on this coil of rope."

No sooner had Bettje lain down, however, when a sailor came along and said abruptly, "You better go down to your bunks. We can't have sick ladies getting in our way up here."

"That wasn't a very nice man," Anneken whispered as she did her best to help Bettje down the ladder.

"Maybe not, but I can understand why he doesn't want us in his way," Bettje managed to say. "And really, I'm glad for my blanket." Flopping onto the bunk, she closed her eyes and waited for Father to return.

Freed 71

Chapter Seventeen

Home in the Hay

"Hmm. This place certainly smells like cows," Bettje commented disdainfully as she entered the barn along with the brethren.

"Since this is where Herr Bolger milks his cows, the smell is hardly surprising," Father said quietly.

His voice held a hint of rebuke, and Bettje knew why. She could easily guess what else Father might have said: "We ought to be thankful for shelter while we wait on the *Journeyman's* repairs."

Of course, Bettje was glad they wouldn't have to sleep out in the open. But still—a cow barn! This was quite a step down from being wealthy citizens of Leeuwarden. Why couldn't they have used some of their money to get rooms at an inn here in this village?

Then again, the village was so small, it might not even have an inn. With a sigh of resignation, Bettje settled onto a pile of hay. Anything was better than that awful, smelly ship's hold. And it certainly felt good not to be seasick anymore!

"We're fortunate there's still so much hay in the barn at this time of the summer," Mother commented cheerfully as she arranged some blankets.

Father said, "Pretty soon Herr Bolger will be cutting the new crop of hay. Maybe we can help him with that."

"You mean we'll be here long enough to make hay?" Bettje asked incredulously.

Father looked at her. "Captain Nordstrom told me the ship's damage is more extensive than he realized. He said it's a miracle we made it to this harbor."

"Oh," said Bettje. Feeling subdued, she recalled how the brethren had prayed as the *Journeyman* limped toward the Friesian shore. Had those prayers actually helped?

Refreshing sleep came to all during that first night in the hay shed. They awoke the next morning to the sound of cows being herded into the adjacent stable. Soon Uncle Leonhard and a few others—including Hannah, who was a farm girl—were over in the stable, helping with the milking.

"It looks like we will have things to do while we are here," Aunt Gertrude commented happily. "The Bolgers also have a large vegetable garden. We womenfolk can surely help with that."

Behind her aunt's back, Bettje made a face. Milking cows! Messing around in a garden! To a city girl the thought was not appealing.

And so, the first few days when some of the other women went off to work in the Bolgers' garden, Bettje claimed she still needed to recover from seasickness. "Besides, somebody has to make meals," she pointed out. Over an open fire behind the barn, meals were being cooked for the entire group.

Sunday morning found the brethren assembled for worship in the hay shed. Bettje felt apprehensive as she took her seat with the others. If Father was now their minister, would he be preaching today? And if he did, would it be the truth? He had not been educated as a priest.

What did he know about the Bible?

Father read a portion of Scripture that he called "the second epistle of John." Bettje had never heard of it, but it sounded like a letter someone would write to a friend. This was the verse upon which Father focused: *For the truth's sake, which dwelleth in us, and shall be with us forever* (II John 2).

"Some have asked me," Father said, speaking slowly, "how the brethren can know that their way is of the truth. The answer is simple. If we rightly believe in Christ, He dwells in us—and He is the truth. That is why John says that the truth dwells in us. And that is why, no matter where we go or who we meet, we will always recognize the truth. We will turn away from Satan's lies. The truth in us is like a magnet that draws us to the truth in others who also have this faith."

Bettje thought, *Father doesn't pretend to understand all about the truth. But he believes the truth lives in him.* The realization, though almost too deep for her fifteen-year-old mind, brought a sense of wonderment to Bettje. And in some strange way, it answered at least part of her questions.

That Monday, Bettje finally gave in and walked with the other girls to the Bolgers' garden. Getting down on her hands and knees, she began pulling weeds. The work was surprisingly pleasant. "Soil isn't really dirty, is it?" she commented to Carla.

"No, it's not. Soil is valuable for growing food," agreed her friend.

"I was so used to buying vegetables at the market that I sometimes forgot they grow in the soil," Bettje admitted sheepishly.

Herr Bolger had a servant named Ursula who occasionally worked in the garden. Ursula was a stout, middle-aged woman who loved to talk. One morning she began in her garrulous way, "Have you heard what happened to those horrible Anabaptists who took over the city of Münster?"

A chill went up Bettje's spine. This woman probably had no idea she was actually speaking to Anabaptists!

Responding to Ursula's question, Aunt Gertrude replied evenly, "We heard that a certain Jan van Leiden took Münster by force, and also that the bishop's troops have laid siege to the city."

"That's right!" Ursula's voice rose in agitation. "Those Anabaptists had forced all Münster's inhabitants to either get rebaptized or leave the city. Jan van Leiden actually proclaimed himself the new King David! He called Münster the center of God's kingdom on earth. Such a sad, deluded affair. And inside Münster, people were starving because no food could get in past the bishop's troops."

Ursula straightened up, while her hands tightened on the shovel. "Anyway, what I was going to tell you—on June 24, the bishop's troops finally won. Jan van Leiden's army was defeated. I sure don't blame the emperor for cracking down on Anabaptists. Why, if no one tried to stop them, they would overrun Germany and the Netherlands!"

Bettje peeked across the carrot row at Aunt Gertrude. She looked very sad. Neither she nor any of the other women offered a reply to Ursula's tirade against the Anabaptists.

Chapter Eighteen

Found Out!

"Who's that yellow-haired girl coming to the garden with Ursula?" Bettje whispered to Hannah one morning as they picked beans together.

"I don't know, but we'll probably find out soon," her friend whispered back.

From the front of the garden they heard Ursula telling the other women, "This is my daughter Mariken. She wanted to come meet you all."

Bettje whispered to Hannah, "It never occurred to me that Herr Bolger's servant is a mother."

"Oh, yes, she's married to one of the stable hands," Hannah responded.

Mariken turned out to be a very friendly child. Up and down the rows she skipped, making sure she met each one of the refugee women and girls. When she came to where Bettje and Hannah were working, Mariken chirped, "I'm eleven. How old are you?"

Chuckling, Bettje told her, "I'm almost sixteen," and Hannah said that she was seventeen.

Squinting at Bettje, Mariken went on, "My mother thinks you're Anabaptists. Is that true?"

Horror shot through Bettje. So Ursula had guessed! With her talkative tongue, the news would soon be all over the village.

Desperately Bettje tried to think how she could keep this from becoming "news." "Mariken, I don't know where your mother picked up such an idea."

The child tossed her head. "Oh, Mother has ways of finding things out! Is it true, then? Because I've never seen a real Anabaptist before."

Hannah spoke up. "We're not Anabaptists. We're just people who believe in Jesus."

Mariken's eyes widened. "Oh? Well, so are we." And off she hopped across the rows toward her mother.

"I spoke the truth, you know," Hannah whispered to Bettje. "My father says our baptism as babies isn't a real baptism at all."

Bettje nodded absently. Hannah's answer had satisfied Mariken—but that didn't mean it would satisfy Ursula. Like a dog sniffing out a trail, she would not stop until she had the information she sought.

When Bettje saw her own mother walking away from the garden, she exclaimed, "I'll go and help her get dinner." Panting, she caught up with Mother. "Do you know what Mariken told us? Ursula thinks we're Anabaptists!"

Mother gave her a quizzical little smile. "Well, I suppose we are—even though we don't agree to that name."

"Yes, but Mother, what will happen if the villagers find out? Will they drive us away? Or put us in prison?" Bettje asked urgently.

"I don't know." Mother seemed very calm.

"I wish the sailors would finish repairing the *Journeyman*," Bettje fretted. "I wish we could get out of here before people start making life hard for us."

Found Out!

Mother said, "It might be a while yet. Captain Nordstrom told Father it's hard to find the wood he needs for the repairs. This little place has no ship-builder's yard; and look, there's not a forest in sight!" She swept her arm to take in the wide expanse of flat polders stretching away to the horizon.

"You mean we'll be stuck here for weeks?" Bettje asked in dismay.

"I don't know," Mother said again. "Let's remember to be thankful for what we do have: food and shelter, and people who are treating us fairly. We even have work to do!"

Muttering to herself, Bettje began preparing vegetables for the soup pot. To her it seemed that the crew and passengers of the *Journeyman* were a very unlucky bunch.

The final notes of the hymn died away. Several chickens clucked sleepily. Overhead, a pigeon cooed.

Suddenly the door of the shed burst open. In walked Herr Bolger and three other men!

Herr Bolger's sandy eyebrows shot up. His blue eyes blinked. Turning to his comrades, he said, "I thought this is what we would find. An illegal worship service."

Terror gripped Bettje. Would Herr Bolger take everyone captive?

Herr Bolger's next words took Bettje completely by surprise. "Do you mind if we stay and listen in?"

Bettje watched her father's face. His reply was hesitant. "Yes…you may stay if your hearts desire the truth."

Each of the four men nodded and took seats on the fresh new hay. As Father started preaching, Bettje glanced at the newcomers. Were they really in search of the truth? Or had they come to spy?

The men sat quietly, attentively. Bettje couldn't help wondering what they thought of Father's preaching. To her it sounded very halting, even crude, compared to Obbe Phillips' fluent sermons.

Yet the story Father read from the Scriptures left Bettje deeply touched. A certain ruler's only daughter lay dying. In desperation the ruler—whose name was Jairus—asked Jesus to come and heal the twelve-year-old maiden.

But before Jesus got to the ruler's home, some servants came to say that the maiden had died. "Don't trouble the Master anymore," they advised Jairus.

Jesus heard that. "Fear not!" He said. "Believe only, and she shall be made whole."

Arriving at the house, Jesus found it full of wailing mourners. "Weep not," He rebuked them. "She is not dead, but sleepeth." And those mourners laughed at Jesus! But He sent them all out of the house, and took only a few trusted disciples with Him into the presence of the maiden. Then He grasped the girl's hand and commanded, "Maid, arise."

And her spirit returned into her body. She arose from her bed.

"Today, Jesus still has that power," Father said earnestly. "We are all dead in sin, unless we have partaken of His grace by faith. We need to feel Christ's hand upon us. We need to respond to His royal command: 'Arise!' And by His power we can walk in newness of life."

Chapter Nineteen

Capture

Every week, more and more of the villagers attended the worship meeting in Herr Bolger's barn. Even Captain Nordstrom and some of the crew began coming. Mid-week meetings were held for Bible study, to prepare people for baptism. And one Sunday in August, Father baptized ten people—including Herr Bolger and his wife. But not their servant Ursula.

"Mother, I simply can't understand it," Bettje admitted one day when the two of them were alone. "Why do all these people join the—the brethren, when they know about the emperor's decree? They could all get killed for being baptized."

Mother looked thoughtful. "Father would say, 'The power of Christ is stronger than the power of death.' Jesus has such drawing power, Bettje. Yes, I can understand that you are puzzled. Why should people be drawn to the cross of Christ, which will almost certainly lead to suffering? But it all comes back to this: the kingdom of heaven is not of this world. In fact, it is the opposite of this world.

It turns worldly thinking upside down."

Bettje smiled wryly. "Upside down. Yes, that is how it looks to me."

"Upside down or not, it is the truth," Mother stated firmly.

"But what will the village priest do when he sees his church growing emptier?" Bettje asked.

"We don't know," was all the answer Mother gave her.

On the first Sunday in September, Bettje's fears were realized. Leering in scorn, the village officials broke in upon the brethren's meeting. They marched up to Father, shackled his hands, and led him away. "We cannot let you take over our village the way Jan van Leiden took Münster!" they said loudly.

Mary and Anneken, the two youngest Claessen girls, began to cry. They had once seen their own father being led away like this.

And Andrew Claessen had not come back.

Bettje sat frozen with fear and horror. Would the officials come back for more prisoners? Would everyone end up captive?

Minutes passed. The congregation seemed to relax. Bernhard gave out a hymn, and they closed the service with fervent singing. No one seemed very hungry for the meal, though.

The girls clustered around Mother in a corner of the shed. Tearfully, Anneken asked the question that also lay uppermost in Bettje's mind: would Father be put to death?

"We don't know what will happen." Mother's voice was tender and sad. "Perhaps the authorities only wanted to give us a scare. But girls, we mustn't lose sight of this fact: life on earth is not the only life. Certainly not the best life! Great glory awaits us if we are released from this life."

Bettje's mind refused to accept that thought. She wanted Father. How could the brethren continue on their flight to safety without him? He was the one who knew where they were going, and who was acquainted with someone at the other end.

Or even if they were to stay here in Friesland, how could they exist without Father? Life without him was unthinkable.

Somehow the days passed. For Bettje, each day held a strange mixture of anticipation and dread. Might Father be released today? Or would the family receive news that would plunge them into grief?

"If only," she fretted to Mother one morning as they dug potatoes in the garden, "if only we could have kept things secret, so that people would not have found out about—about the Anabaptism. Then this wouldn't have happened."

"But Bettje," Mother responded slowly, "Father was more at peace this way. He was troubled about keeping our faith a secret. The Bible says that if we deny Christ, He will also deny us."

"But simply trying to be safe—is that denying Him?" Bettje questioned.

Mother picked up one last potato and rose to her feet. "I don't understand everything," she admitted. "But I know Father's conscience felt clear this way. When the church was known and shining like a light to the world, others could be drawn to Christ."

Bettje fell silent. It never worked to argue with Mother. Her answers went above arguments.

"Ladies, I have news for you," said a man's voice nearby. There stood Captain Nordstrom, looking both pleased and perplexed.

Mother clasped her hands. "You have news about Adrian?"

"Yes. I managed to find out where he is, and have spoken to him. He is well, and…" Captain Nordstrom shifted from one foot to the other. "He said to encourage you to keep on trusting."

"We try," breathed Mother.

"Also," the captain went on, "we are finished with our repairs to the ship and would like to sail soon. It is September already. When autumn comes, the Baltic Sea is a place of storms."

That sent a shiver up Bettje's spine. To think of all the tranquil summer weeks they had spent marooned here—and now they would be facing storms.

"Adrian urged us to leave without him," the captain said. "He believes he can eventually follow, perhaps on foot across the German lands. He says he is no stranger to such journeys."

"That is true," said Mother. "He has walked hundreds of miles across the face of Europe."

Bettje stared at Mother. Was she actually agreeing that they should leave without Father? Bettje wanted to scream, "No, no! Not without Father!"

"We don't want to prevent you from continuing with your journey," Mother told Captain Nordstrom. "But if you could give us a day or so, in order to meet and make plans—?"

"Of course," agreed the captain. "Shall I find Leonhard and Bernhard and let them know how things stand?"

"Please do."

That evening found the brethren huddled in the hay shed for a meeting. Included were not only those from Leeuwarden but also the newly baptized ones from the village.

First several of the men led in prayer, asking for God's guidance. Then they discussed Captain Nordstrom's wish to proceed because of storms, and Father's advice that they should go. Bettje felt her mind growing numb. She could tell that the brethren were considering it. They actually thought the group could go on without their leader!

"And is there room on the ship for a few more?" questioned Jakob, one of the Friesian brethren. "If we stay here, our families will hardly be safe, since it looks like the village officials plan to enforce the emperor's decree."

"We'll need to ask the captain about that," replied Leonhard. "I do know that some bales of wool became soggy due to the water the ship took in. Those bales have been thrown out. Perhaps the captain will be glad to take on a few more paying passengers."

Herr Bolger looked at his wife. "We will stay—and may the Lord help us to be a small beacon for the truth right here."

Capture

"We will stay too," said another of the Friesian brethren. "But it tears our hearts to see you go, because we feel small and weak. We don't know if we can uphold the faith like we should."

Bernhard reminded him warmly, "God's power is available to help. Also, as soon as we can we will write Obbe Phillips and ask him to visit you. Every local church needs leaders."

"If you go, we feel our leaders are leaving us," Johann Bolger said brokenly.

"Perhaps you feel like the Ephesian elders did when they took leave of the Apostle Paul at Miletus." Bernhard paged the Bible as if looking for a certain passage. "It says here that the sorrowful elders all followed Paul down to the ship, knowing they would see his face no more. This is what Paul said to comfort them: 'And now, brethren, I commend you to God, and to the word of his grace, which is able to build you up, and to give you an inheritance among all them that are sanctified'" (Acts 20:32).

Chapter Twenty

Strong Rock

The next morning, Jan was the first down the hatch. Bettje stood on deck, forlornly watching him disappear down the ladder. How she hated the thought of descending again into that smelly hold!

Suddenly from below echoed Jan's surprised voice. "Father! How did you get here?"

Mother pushed past Bettje and groped for the ladder. After her tumbled Bettje and the Claessen girls. There on the bunk sat Father, so happy that tears were running down his cheeks!

Nor were his the only tears. When everyone had finally calmed down, Father explained, "We ought to thank God for Captain Nordstrom. He's the one who managed to free me last night. Just how he did it is not clear to me. I got the feeling the captain doesn't want to talk about it. So we won't pester him; we'll just be thankful."

"That won't be hard," Mother said feelingly.

Soon they sensed the ship lifting and straining beneath their feet, and they knew the wind was in the sails. Northward and westward they sailed, causing Jan to ask a bewildered question: "But isn't the Vistula River east of here?"

"It is, but Captain Nordstrom wants to stay well clear of Denmark. No more getting stuck on shoals if he can help it! That's why we're sailing somewhat to the west just now. But soon we'll veer eastward to enter the Skagerrak," explained Father.

"What's the Skagerrak?" wondered Titus.

"It's the arm of the North Sea that flows in between the coasts of Denmark and Norway," came the reply. "I should try to draw a map for you." With the lantern flickering wildly as the ship rode the waves, Father scratched out a crude map on a piece of board.

"Here is Denmark, jutting up into the North Sea like a fat thumb," Father pointed out. "And here is Norway, looking like an enormous caterpillar with its mouth wide open, ready to swallow the thumb of Denmark."

That brought chuckles from the young people clustered around him. He went on, "Now this is the Skagerrak; we sail up here, right into the caterpillar's mouth, then we turn sharply eastward into the strait called the Kattegat, which goes down Denmark's east coast."

He looked up at Jan. "You were up on deck a few minutes ago. I suppose there's no land in sight?"

"No. None at all."

"That's just as the captain wants it—for now. But once we enter the Skagerrak, you young people are in for a surprise. You've spent your lives on the flat polders of the Netherlands. Norway's coast is unlike anything you've ever seen!"

"Tell me what it's like," Bettje coaxed.

"Since you have never seen rocks, I hardly know how to describe it. Can you imagine land that rises straight up into the sky—like a very high dike?"

Bettje blinked. Land—going straight up! Her imagination was not equal to the task. "I guess I'll have to wait till I see it."

But unfortunately, Bettje grew seasick again. So did most of the other girls. Most of the men stayed well; the interval on the Friesian coast had cured them, and now they could tread the restless ship like seasoned sailors.

A hand grasped Bettje's shoulder, and a voice urged, "Surely you want to see those rocks, Bettje. We're off the coast of Norway now. I could help you up the ladder!"

Bettje opened her eyes to find Carla peering at her. "I thought you were sick," she croaked.

"Well, I was. But Titus persuaded me to go up on deck, and I'm not sorry I did. It made me feel better! Won't you try it too?"

Digging in her elbows, Bettje managed to get her head off the pillow. Then she sank back again, groaning, "I don't think I can do it. I must be sicker than you were."

"At first I also thought I couldn't do it. But Titus made it sound so interesting—Norway's coast, I mean—that I tried again. Bettje, I simply have no words to describe those rocks. They're—they're—" Carla spread her hands helplessly. Then she coaxed one more time, "Won't you try again? It'll make you feel better. I'm almost sure of it."

And so, with Carla pushing from below and Hannah pulling from above, Bettje toiled up the ladder. The moment her head came above deck she gasped, "What's that?"

It looked like a wall—or a dike. A jagged, rocky dike rising up from the waves and nearly blotting out the northern sky. Snow clung to crevices among the boulders. In shades of blue, gray and white, the cliffs were so beautiful that they stunned Bettje into awed silence.

"Here, sit down on these ropes," Jan offered.

"But—but the sailors won't like it if I do that," she protested.

Hannah urged, "We'll help you get out of the way if necessary. Come on. Sit down and enjoy the view."

So Bettje took a seat on that pile of coarse hempen rope and rested her forehead against the spray-damp railing. Ever changing, yet always the same, Norway's rocky cliffs sped by as the ship scudded through the Skagerrak.

Standing nearby, Father asked softly, "Did you know that in the Bible, God is often called a Rock?"

When Bettje shook her head, Father quoted, "'For thou art my rock and my fortress; therefore for thy name's sake lead me and guide me.' That's from the Psalms. David also says, 'Bow down thine ear to me; deliver me speedily: be thou my strong rock, for an house of defense to save me.'" (From Psalm 31).

Eyes on those snowy crags, Bettje nodded slowly. Never had she seen anything more majestic, more deserving of that comparison with God Himself. Those towering rocks spoke of strength, and surely God was strong. Strong enough to guard a whole shipload of people adrift on the North Sea.

But the hardest question for Bettje was not whether God was strong. The hardest question was: did this mean the God of the Catholics, the "holy mother church"? Or did it mean the God of the brethren, with their simple, direct faith?

Chapter Twenty-One

Cleft of the Rock

Bettje screamed as her head hit the floorboards. A giant unseen hand had lifted her up and flung her from the bunk. This was worse than a nightmare. It was real! She really was lying face-down on the filthy floor.

Groaning, Bettje picked herself up. Instantly that same "hand" threw her down again. The ship heaved and bucked beneath her like a living thing. Children cried. A roar of wind and water drummed in Bettje's ears.

"It's a storm," she heard Father saying. "Storms in the Kattegat Strait can be fierce this time of year."

Hurtling down from the Norwegian steeps, the storm had torn the sails to shreds before the sailors could reef them in. The ship floundered helplessly. One moment she climbed high upon a wave-crest, and the next she plunged into a deep trough. Seawater washed across the deck and leaked into the hold.

"Lie down again, Bettje." That was Father's voice, calm and steady.

"Hold on to this post. Now I'm going to rig a kind of harness that will keep you in bed despite the storm." With bedding and ropes, he secured her to the bunk.

He smiled at her. "Some of the children didn't like being tied down. But they find out it's better than being thrown around like a rag doll."

Bettje's teeth chattered uncontrollably. "H-how l-long will this storm last?"

"Oh, I don't know. Some of these Baltic Sea storms last only a day or two," Father answered brightly.

"You mean it might last a whole day?" Bettje almost shrieked.

"Yes. That's why we're tying everyone down." Father's steady gaze held her eyes. "The Bible says, 'Be still and know that I am God.' Deep down in our hearts, we can be still even in the wildest storm."

Bettje wanted to retort, "I don't know what you're talking about." But instead she shut her mouth and gritted her teeth as another gigantic wave smashed into the ship.

Then from the direction of the Claessen girls' bunk came a tremulous song: "Peace, be still. Peace, be still." It was the same song they had sung the night the dikes were leaking. On they forged with the hymn, even when the words were jerked from their mouths by the ship's convulsions.

How can they do it? Bettje asked herself. *How can they possibly sing at a time like this?*

Other voices joined in. "Lord of the waves and the sea… At thy command they cease… May we rest in the sheltered Rock… And there, in the storm, find peace."

In spite of her misery, Bettje's mind formed a picture. She could see a tall, solid Rock, immovable through the ages; and she could see huge waves that pounded in futile rage against that Rock. High up above the frothing waves, the Rock had a cleft—and there, safe in spite of the storm, huddled a group of people.

Oh, if only she too could reach that cleft!

At last some feeble rays of daylight trickled through the cracks high up on the ship's side. But daylight did not diminish the storm. On it raged, tossing the ship up and down its billows.

Though himself securely lashed to his bunk, Father managed to reach his Bible. In between the ship's worst plunges, he began to tell a story. He kept consulting the Bible, but Bettje could tell that the account was in his own words.

"In Acts 27 we read of a journey made by the Apostle Paul on a stormy sea. This was the Mediterranean Sea, not the Baltic Sea; and Paul was on his way to Rome, in Italy. Having been taken captive by the Jews, Paul traveled as a prisoner under a Roman guard. Just like the *Journeyman*, this ship had started off rather late in the sailing season. Stormy winds blew them to an island called Crete, where the ship managed to enter a port called Fair Havens.

"'We ought to stay here for the winter,' Paul urged the ship's captain. 'If we continue, we will run into trouble.'

"But the captain was in no mood to take advice from a mere prisoner. Right then the weather seemed balmy. So he decided to lift anchor and move on along the coast of Crete to a bigger harbor where the sailors could enjoy the winter at a large city.

"That was a big mistake! Just as the ship left the harbor's protection, a terrific storm came down from the northwest. This type of storm was so common that the natives had a name for it: Euroclydon. The Bible says: 'And when the ship was caught, and could not bear up into the wind, we let her drive' (Acts 27:15).

"What now? Would Eurocydon blow the ship right across the sea to be wrecked on the coast of Africa? Fortunately, the ship entered a calm spot on the lee side of an island. Taking advantage of this calm, the sailors did all they could to reinforce the ship. Then they threw any unnecessary tackle overboard. And they set the sails in such a way that, hopefully, Euroclydon would carry them toward Italy. If only the wind would die down, there was a possibility that they would make it to safety.

"So there was the ship, pitching and swaying across the waves—" Bettje shrieked as the *Journeyman* took a steep nosedive. The ship's timbers groaned and creaked. How long could a ship endure such punishment?

"—for fourteen long days and nights," Father continued. "Neither sun nor stars could be seen because storm clouds covered the sky. The sailors did not know where they were. Most of them had given up all hope.

"At that point, Paul stood up to speak. Imagine him on that storm-tossed deck, with the captain and crew clustered around him. 'You should have listened to me, and never left Fair Havens,' Paul began. 'But be of good cheer! Last night there came to me an angel of God, whose I am, and whom I serve.'" Father paused. "May we all say that of the Lord: 'Whose I am, and whom I serve.' In Him we are safe."

Safe? thought Bettje, nearly wrenched from her harness by the force of a wave. *Do you call this safe, Father?* But she did not say it out loud.

Oblivious to his daughter's thoughts, Father went on: "There on that storm-driven ship, Paul assured the crew, 'I believe God, that it shall be even as it was told me.' (Acts 27:25). 'In due time we shall be cast on an island.'

"I don't know what the sailors thought as they listened to Paul. I don't know if they believed him. But soon after that, they realized that land was near. Their depth-soundings showed it. So they quickly cast some anchors in hopes that this would prevent the ship from being wrecked on the shore.

"That happened around midnight. As dawn broke, Paul urged the crew, 'You haven't eaten for days. Now eat some bread to regain your strength for the struggle that lies ahead.' And there in the presence of them all, Paul gave thanks to God, broke bread and began to eat.

The Bible says, 'They were all of good cheer, and they also took some meat.'

"What a beautiful picture we have there!" Father exclaimed. "Overhead the skies are dark. Beneath are the roiling waves. Water washes over the heaving deck. But Paul stands there calmly breaking bread, and handing out the pieces to the crew.

"I can't help but think of Jesus, on the night before His crucifixion. He too was facing a terrific storm; soon He would sweat blood in the garden as He submitted to the Father's will. Yes, he calmly broke bread with his disciples.

"This is the message for us: no matter what dangers beset us, let's 'be of good cheer, and take meat.' God's Word is our 'meat' to strengthen us, whatever befalls."

Chapter Twenty-Two

Not Far From the Kingdom

Eventually the storm subsided. Though the ship still rolled and heaved, those agonizing plunges grew less. Father went up to speak with the captain. Upon his return he reported, "Abel is amazed that the *Journeyman* has survived. He thinks it must be because of our prayers. I told him it's not so much our prayers as the power of the One to whom we pray."

"How long till we reach the Vistula?" Jan wondered.

"Only a few more days, if all goes well," Father replied with a smile. "Before we can make much headway, the crew needs to repair some sails."

Then another danger appeared on the horizon. Bettje's first inkling of this new danger came when she noticed a pair of strange boots hastily descending the ladder—expensive leather boots such as none of the brethren owned.

They belonged to the captain. Standing in the dim, reeking hold, he burst out, "Where's Adrian?"

"Here." Looking very surprised, Father sat up in his bunk... Whoever heard of a captain visiting his passengers in the hold?

"Pirates," Abel croaked. "A pirate ship is closing in on us. I can tell by the flag flying from the masthead."

Bettje felt herself turn cold. Anyone could see that Abel Nordstrom was terrified—simply terrified.

"What do you expect will happen?" Father asked quietly.

"They will come alongside and train their guns on us. That ship is bristling with guns. And we have only two." Abel reached out a hand to steady himself against a post. "I've heard stories of pirates who come aboard and either kill everybody, or—or take them captive." His eyes flitted to the girls, then back to Father. "Some of my sailors have handguns or swords. We could try to put up a fight...but we haven't a chance." Abel swallowed hard. "I came down here to—to ask what you think we should do."

Father looked around at the other men. Then he asked Abel, "Do you honestly want to do it Christ's way?"

Abel spread his hands in a despairing gesture. "I've no choice, really. If we try to fight them, we're doomed. But...but...God has protected you thus far. Why should He abandon you now?"

"We only pray that God's will may be done," said Bernhard.

Father nodded. "And His perfect will does not include taking swords to defend ourselves. When the officers came to take Jesus captive for His crucifixion, one of His disciples drew out a sword. But Jesus bade him return the sword to its sheath. Abel, you could welcome the pirates aboard. Offer them food. And money. We have some money we could give. Let them plunder your goods."

Abel's fists clenched. "You—you are asking a great deal."

"Well, you wanted advice."

The captain ducked his head. "I must go up and talk to the crew. Pray, please."

So all who could, knelt beside their bunks. Father and the other men took turns praying.

Bettje listened in bewilderment. Yes, there were a few short petitions for protection. But mostly the prayers were for the souls of the pirates, and also the souls of Abel and his crew. "May they come to You and know the truth," was the way Father put it.

Bettje lay shuddering beneath her filthy blanket. Any minute, gunshots might ring out. Fierce strangers might clamber into the hold… Desperately, she strove to close her mind to these thoughts.

Soon they heard strange voices shouting. Something bumped and scraped against the ship. A torrent of footsteps rattled overhead.

A crew member hurtled down the ladder. "M-more money, " he pleaded, his teeth chattering. "The captain offered food to the pirates, so right now they're eating. But they say they must have more money than what the captain has given them."

Swiftly the brethren dug in their chests and filled a pouch with coins. Stammering his thanks, the sailor flew back up the ladder.

The voices continued. Some were loud and argumentative. Some sounded low and frightened. Then, after more stomping, bumping and scraping, the ship grew silent.

Bettje drew a tremulous breath. "Do you think they're really gone?"

"Sounds pretty quiet up there," responded Father.

The hatch opened. Another pair of feet started down the ladder—feet clad only in ragged socks.

It was the captain. A jubilant smile covered his face. "They're off and away! Nobody's hurt! Your advice worked."

"We only told you what the Bible says," Father reminded him.

Abel nodded. "That pirate captain kept saying he wants more money. When I said I have no more, he scowled. That's when I remembered something I learned during Bible study in Friesland. Didn't Jesus say that if a man takes your coat, then give him your cloak as well? So I took off my coat and my boots, and handed them to the pirate captain."

"Indeed, that is the way of Christ," Father agreed.

"You should have seen the look on the pirate's face," Abel chortled. "I couldn't describe it if I tried. Pretty soon he turned to his men and said, 'We better get going.'"

"Coals of fire," murmured Uncle Leonhard. "You were heaping coals of fire on his head."

When Abel gave him a quizzical look, Leonhard reached for the Bible. It says here in Romans 12:20, 'Therefore if thine enemy hunger, feed him; if he thirst, give him drink: for in so doing thou shalt heap coals of fire on his head.'"

"Ah, I see," Abel said thoughtfully. "Your way—what you call the way of Christ—it is contrary to the world's way."

"Jesus said His kingdom is not of this world," Father told him.

Abel turned abruptly toward the ladder. "Now we must reach port with all possible speed. Our supplies are very low." Up through the hatch disappeared the ragged socks.

"I wonder if my shoes would fit him," mused Bernhard.

"Or mine," added Father. Then, in a pleased voice, he continued, "That man is not far from the kingdom of God."

Chapter Twenty-Three

Gdansk Harbor

"I hate these biscuits! They're so hard and dry, I can't even chew them," complained Bettje. Petulantly she flung the biscuit away. It fell to the floor and rolled a short distance before coming to rest in a puddle of foul seawater.

"Bettje." Mother's voice, though low, was full of reproach. She stooped to pick up the biscuit. "There's almost no food left on the ship. We mustn't waste any. Shall I soak part of this biscuit in water for you? That would soften it up."

Frowning, Bettje shook her head. "I'm not hungry. Not for a biscuit anyway. At first when we left Friesland, we had potatoes and carrots and turnips…" Her voice trailed off. What good was it to wish for things they no longer had? Why yearn for the teeming market of Leeuwarden, with its stalls full of fruits and vegetables? Here in the middle of the Baltic Sea, such things were only a dream.

Mother's reproachful eyes were still upon her. Bettje burst out, "I'm just so sick of—of being sick! I'm sick of everything!"

"Eating something might make you feel better," Mother said.

Once again, Bettje pushed away the biscuit. She watched as Mother offered it to Carla, who accepted it and began chewing. Bettje swallowed hard. Had Carla seen that biscuit landing in the bilge water? How could she be so meek and uncomplaining?

Deep inside Bettje, a voice whispered, *It's probably because Carla is a child of God. That's just how the brethren all are—never complaining, always cheerful.*

Disconsolate, Bettje lay back against her pillow. Part of her longed to be like that too. But how could she ever be meek and submissive enough to become such a child of God? Bettje did not feel meek and submissive at all. She felt weary, and wretched, and rebellious, and—and sick. Sick of it all. Why, oh why had the Weaver family ever left Leeuwarden? Why had Father and Mother allowed themselves to be attracted by the brethren? Endless "whys" tumbled through her mind.

The hatch opened, and Jan backed down the ladder. "Land has been sighted!" he announced jubilantly. "Captain Nordstrom says we'll soon be rounding the cape and heading into the Gulf of Gdansk."

"Land," said Bettje, almost unbelievingly. Could it be true? Would she soon have solid ground beneath her feet again?

Jan turned to his sister. "Will you come up to have a look?"

Bettje sighed. "I would like to, but Jan, I think I'd better save my energy for when it's time to leave the ship. Climbing that ladder still looks like a big chore to me."

"I wonder why you're so much sicker than the others," her brother said worriedly.

"I'll get well once my feet hit the ground," she promised, more jauntily than she felt.

A day later, the ship docked at Gdansk. "This is certainly a busy port!" Jan reported enthusiastically to his sister after spending some time on deck. "There are ships of all sizes, though a lot of them have docked for the winter, so the harbor itself is not very busy. Gdansk must be a huge city. You should see all the buildings!"

Father said, "I've heard that among the cities of Europe, Gdansk is second in size only to Amsterdam."

Jan let out a low whistle. "Amsterdam has been called the 'hub of the world' because of all the trade going through its docks. If Gdansk is comparable to that, it must be really big! I wonder what cargoes all these ships will carry, come spring."

"A lot of farm products," Father told him. "The Vistula Delta is a good place for grain growing. And much of the grain goes to Amsterdam. Can you guess why?"

Jan thought for a moment. "I guess it would take a lot of wheat to feed a city the size of Amsterdam."

"Right. Then there's flax. Much flax is raised here in Poland, then shipped as raw materials to places like Belgium and Friesland where a lot of weaving is done. Some of these Polish-German noblemen own huge farms. And that's why we'll be able to find homes here. Those farms are in desperate need of workers."

"I thought you said we'll be doing drainage work," Jan said.

"That, too. Count Frankfurt, the man I'm acquainted with, owns acres of marshland along the Vistula that he'd like to reclaim."

"Is he the one who invited you to move here?" wondered Samuel.

"Yes. He said he needs someone with a knowledge of dike building."

"How soon will we get to this Frankfurt's place?" wondered Adam, the youngest of the Claessen boys.

Father stroked his beard thoughtfully. "I'm not sure. The Frankfurt estate is a little way up the river. I'd hoped Captain Nordstrom would sail right up there, but he says he doesn't dare. He thinks we ought to find a smaller river boat to make the trip. You see, the waters of the Vistula are quite low in the fall."

Titus seemed puzzled. "Why would a river be low in the autumn?"

"The way I understand it, there are two high-water seasons for the

Vistula. One is in the spring, when the ice is melting. And the other is in the summer. Apparently a lot of rain falls during the summer up in the hills where the Vistula has its source. Sometimes the floods are bad enough to damage crops. Count Frankfurt has big plans for dike building and canal digging to control those floods."

Jan looked at Titus. "I can hardly wait to get to work. Sitting around on a ship with nothing to do gets pretty boring."

"Sure does," agreed his friend.

Listening in, Bettje thought mournfully, *If only I would feel so energetic! But I can hardly even lift my head from the pillow. How will I ever climb that ladder when the time comes to leave this hold?*

As though guessing her thoughts, Father glanced across at Bettje. "Once Abel lets me off this ship, I'm going to find a market where I can buy some vegetables. Then we'll make a soup that not even Bettje can resist!"

"Sounds good," she said weakly. Her arms and hands had grown gaunt, and her legs looked like sticks. The last while she had eaten so little that it was hard to imagine her stomach even tolerating food again.

But the next day at noon, Bettje awoke from a doze to find a tempting aroma tickling her nostrils. There beside her bunk was a steaming pot of turnip soup, with slices of potatoes, carrots and onions! "Oooh," she breathed as Mother ladled some into a bowl. The first spoonful tasted so good that she was sorry to swallow it. But soon she took a second spoonful, then another and another.

"Perhaps you'd better not eat too much at first," Mother cautioned.

Bettje clutched her stomach. "No, better not! Will there be more soup for supper?"

"There certainly will be," Mother assured her.

Chapter Twenty-Four

Almost Home

Meanwhile, Father had found a man with a boat who agreed to take them up the Vistula. "Bettje, do you think you'll feel ready to travel tomorrow morning? The man would like to get an early start," he said.

"Yes, if you can get me up that ladder," Bettje responded wryly.

"We'll rig up a sling and lift you out," Father promised.

Bettje stared. "You don't even think I can climb up by myself?"

Father glanced at Mother, who said, "Bettje, maybe you don't realize how sick you've been. It will take a while for you to recover. In the meantime, we want to take good care of you."

"But—but—surely I can walk!" sputtered Bettje, watching the other girls come nimbly down the ladder after a tour on deck.

Mother laid a hand on her arm. "Perhaps soon. But for now, you must do as we say. Bettje…" She paused, trying to control her emotions. "For a while there, we thought we might lose you. But now that you're eating again, things will come all right."

Bettje lay silent, trying to take this in. Had she really been that sick? So sick that her parents thought she would die?

She smiled slowly. "Well, I'm ready to get out of this ship—even if it takes a sling to manage!"

The other women got busy, making sure that their belongings were packed in bundles. When morning came, all was in readiness. And down through the hatch swung a piece of leather fastened to ropes. Jan called down gaily, "Bettje, do you want the first ride on this sling?"

"Let's send up some bundles first," Father suggested. "That'll give the young fellows some practice in operating the sling."

Bettje's stomach churned as she watched several bundles teetering up the hatch. Beside her, Lela asked softly, "Are you scared?"

"I shouldn't be, after weathering the Baltic Sea," Bettje said, trying to laugh. Turning to Mother, she wheedled, "Are you sure I mayn't try climbing the ladder?"

"Quite sure," Mother replied firmly. "Here, I'll help you sit on the sling. Now we'll make this band fast under your arms. You can't fall out. Just hold onto this rope."

So Bettje clung with all her might. Her head spun from sitting upright. With a lurch, the sling started toward the hatch—and before Bettje could stop it, a shriek burst from her lips.

"Did we frighten you?" Jan asked apologetically once she sat safely on deck.

Embarrassed, Bettje answered, "I'm sorry. I don't know why I screamed."

"Was that ride even worse than those big waves on the Baltic?" Samuel asked teasingly.

"Not worse. Just—different." With all her heart, Bettje wished the boys would stop talking about it.

Perhaps Carla sensed that, for she asked quickly, "So what do you think of Gdansk, Bettje?"

Wonderingly she ran her eyes from the teeming docks to the ranks of buildings rising above the shore. City girl though she was, this place quite took her breath away. "It's huge!" she whispered.

"Thousands of people must live here," said Lela. "And look at all the ships in the harbor!"

Masts towered from vessels of all shapes and sizes. Grain barges and lumber barges made their ponderous way across the water. How busy and prosperous everything seemed!

When it was time to go ashore, Bettje faced another trial. Along came Father, Leonhard, Bernhard and Jakob, carrying a stretcher! "This is for you," Father told Bettje. "Can you stand on your feet for a bit? Then I'll help you lie down on this stretcher."

Bettje wanted to protest. She wanted to say that she could walk. But the moment she stood up, everything around her seemed to spin in circles. So instead of protesting, she lay meekly on the stretcher and allowed the men to carry her down the gangplank.

"We're going along the docks for a short distance till we get to Emil's boat," Father explained, looking down at Bettje. "So just enjoy your ride."

She tried. But oh, she was so very tired of anything that rocked or swayed—and the stretcher certainly did both as the men threaded their way among the dockworkers.

At last, at last the stretcher stopped. "Please, may I stand up?" Bettje pleaded. "I want to feel the solid ground beneath my feet for just a little bit before I have to board a boat again."

"All right," said Father. "But take it easy."

Slowly she touched one foot to a solid plank of the dock. Then the other foot. "Aaah," she breathed. "It really is solid! It holds still!"

She stood up. Everything whirled around her.

Down she dropped onto the stretcher again. "So now when I've reached solid ground at last," she said, smiling weakly, "it's me that is swaying!"

"You'll be better soon," Father soothed. "Here comes Mother now, with the other girls. And this is the boat that will take us upriver. Good morning, Emil." Speaking in German, Father greeted a stocky man with a grizzled beard.

"Good morning," came the brisk reply. "Is everybody here? Then we will load up and set sail."

"Can all of us fit into that boat?" Anneken asked incredulously. Compared to the *Journeyman*, the boat certainly looked small. But Father reminded everyone that this trip would only last a few hours.

"Surely we can stand it for that long to be packed in like sardines," he urged.

As the men carried her aboard, Bettje fretted, "Won't this stretcher take up too much room?"

"There's a place reserved for it," Father told her.

Bettje smiled weakly. Strange, but it made her feel right at home when the boat rose and fell in the water. She quickly fell asleep as the vessel glided upstream.

"You're missing a lot of scenery!" Hannah's voice spoke in Bettje's ear.

So she wrenched her eyes open. Wide brown fields stretched away from the Vistula's banks. "Looks like—like the Netherlands," Bettje commented. "Low and flat."

"Marshy, too, in some places," Mother informed her. "Up ahead is a castle. Must be some nobleman's estate. Look at all the buildings!"

"What are those queer structures near the river?" Jan wanted to know.

"Grain storage. From there, the grain is loaded right onto the river barges," Father said. His eyes searched the river. "If I remember correctly, the next castle we come to will be Count Frankfurt's."

"Then we're almost home," Mother said softly.

Almost Home

Chapter Twenty-Five

Interrogation

From his position at the helm, Emil the boatman looked down at Father. "So do you want me to wait here until you've talked to Count Frankfurt? Maybe he'll say he can't keep you."

"From what he said when I spoke to him last year, I don't think there'll be a problem," Father answered confidently. "Besides, we have no options. By the time we've paid you for this fare, we'll be out of money."

Lying on her stretcher in the stern, Bettje let out a gasp. Out of money! But Father had been such a wealthy man.

Then she remembered the pouch that had been filled with coins to satisfy the pirates' demands. No doubt that was where Father's money had gone.

As the first people began to scramble over the gunwales to shore, Bettje gazed up the hill. There stood the Frankfurt castle, its ramparts gleaming gold and amber in the setting sun. Beyond the castle sprawled a variety of buildings. Unless Count Frankfurt had a very large family, he would surely have room for these ten refugee families landing on his dock.

Two guards popped from a small building near the dock. "Who comes here?" one of them demanded, shaking his long spear.

From shore, Bernhard called back to the boat, "Adrian! This man wants to talk to you."

Seconds later Father stood before the menacing guards. Heart in her throat, Bettje listened to the soldiers' rapid-fire German. She could not understand all they said, but obviously they were challenging Father's right to be here.

So Father told them in his halting German how he had met with Count Frankfurt last year. "He gave me to understand that he needs workers for his many acres—especially workers with knowledge of dikes and drainage. I belonged to the Water Authority in Leeuwarden. Count Frankfurt gave me a warm invitation to come, along with any others who cared to work for him."

The guards stared, silent and suspicious. Finally the one said something to the other, who then told Father, "You may come. But don't be surprised if you get turned away."

It was horrible, climbing from that boat under the hostile stares of those guards. To Bettje it seemed that they looked at her with extra malevolence. No doubt they wondered what good a sick girl on a stretcher would be to their master!

Swaying and jerking, the stretcher bore her up the hill. Having accompanied the straggling line of refugees, the one guard smote his spear on the castle gate and yelled, "Open!"

Next came more suspicious stares and more questions as other guards confronted them. Tears of anxiety and weariness spilled over Bettje's cheeks. Was there no more kindness to be found in all the world for these pitiful outcasts from the Netherlands?

Suddenly a voice exclaimed, "Adrian Weaver! You have come!" There stood a man in a splendid uniform—unmistakably the Count himself. He wrung Father's hand warmly. Abashed, the guards melted out of sight.

At first Bettje felt encouraged by the Count's warm welcome. But then his eyes, too, traveled over the soiled, ragged group on his doorstep—and those eyes were full of questions. Especially when they lingered on Bettje's stretcher.

"Do you bring infectious diseases?" Count Frankfurt demanded abruptly. "Because last year we had some refugees fleeing from the Turks, and they brought a disease that spread among our workers. Killed off dozens of them."

Bettje shivered. The story of disease was bad enough. But the Count's manner was even worse. He made it sound as though his workers were of little more value than livestock.

Father replied respectfully, "There are no infectious diseases that we're aware of. My daughter became so ill from seasickness that she is still recovering."

"I suppose that could happen," the Count agreed gruffly. "Now tell me this. Are there others besides yourself who can do drainage work?"

"Every one of the men is willing," Father replied.

Count Frankfurt nodded with satisfaction. "That is good. I have a plan all mapped out for many ditches and dikes. The more digging we get done this fall, the better. The river is at its lowest right now. Come spring, we'll be glad for every ditch that's been dug."

Bettje sighed inwardly. This man could probably keep on talking all night about his favorite subject of drainage. Couldn't he see how tired and hungry these people were?

Only one baby whimpered as the Count rambled on, describing his problems with spring ice jams and summer floods. At last he said, "I'll have to ask my steward about room for all you people. You've eaten, I suppose?"

"Not since this morning before we entered the boat," Father told him.

The Count's eyebrows shot up. "So! You need food as well." He did not sound happy. "The thing is, I don't know if we've laid by enough provender for so many people this winter."

"I'm sorry. We left the Netherlands rather suddenly, and had no way of letting you know that we're coming," Father apologized.

The Count's eyes narrowed. "Suddenly, you say? Any reasons in particular why you left?"

Apprehension gnawed at Bettje's stomach. What would Count Frankfurt do when he found out these were Anabaptists? Would he turn them back to the riverbank? But Emil's boat had long since departed.

"We left because of the emperor's decree," Father said. "We serve the Lord in truth, and so have become outcasts from the Roman Catholic Church."

"Ah," said the Count. "Ah, I see. Then you're of the sect called Anabaptists? I've heard of their seditious ways. Was there not one named Matthys who attempted to take Münster by force?"

"We are not of those. Christ commands us to not resist with the sword," Father said. Bettje could tell from his voice that he, too, was very tired. How long must this merciless interrogation continue?

At last Count Frankfurt's face softened. "I'm willing to take you at your word. You look harmless, and I need workers. Wait here while I fetch my steward."

From then on, things happened surprisingly fast. An hour later Bettje lay on the floor of a castle room, her stomach warmed and satisfied with hot soup. In the darkness around her she heard gentle snores as the weary refugees dropped off to sleep.

Chapter Twenty-Six

Offscourings

Bettje stirred restlessly. Now that her strength was returning, she longed to be out working with the other girls. In a nearby shed her friends were busy retting flax. Count Frankfurt's estate had yielded a huge crop of flax this past summer, and he was delighted to have so many women and girls who could prepare the fibers for spinning. Rubbing his hands in satisfaction, the Count had planned, "There's no reason why we shouldn't export the finished product rather than raw flax, now that we have workers to do the job!"

Bettje picked up her knife and began peeling potatoes again. She hated it that her hands still tired so quickly from such a little task. Why couldn't she get well faster? The other girls no longer had any after effects from the sea voyage.

Bettje and her mother were helping the castle servants in the kitchen. After a while the two servants went out. Glad for a chance to be alone with Mother, Bettje began asking the questions that sometimes entered her mind. "Don't you think we should be able to make a lot of money here, Mother? Surely Count Frankfurt will pay the men well for all that hard digging they're doing. And once we get the looms up and running, we women can make money too. We should soon be able to build homes of our own, don't you think?"

Mother did not answer right away. "Why do you ask such questions, Bettje?"

"Well, why shouldn't I?" Bettje retorted. "It's just normal to think of making money, isn't it?"

"In Leeuwarden it was normal. But here…" Mother's voice trailed off.

"Why should things be different here?" Bettje demanded.

"I don't know if I can explain or not, but Father told me that Poland's laws are different from the rest of Europe. In fact, some Polish laws were changed just recently, in the past ten years or so. And they were changed in the favor of noblemen who own huge estates. We told you that the ruler of Poland is King Sigismund, which is true. But the Polish parliament has the real governing power. And the nobles are in control of Parliament!"

"I don't understand," Bettje admitted.

"Well, let's look at the rest of Europe for a bit. In the last generation or so, things have changed dramatically. Years ago it wasn't possible for most people to live in a city and make plenty of money from trade. Either you were a wealthy nobleman, or you were a poor peasant living on a nobleman's land, allowed to keep barely enough of your crops to feed yourself. But these days, the peasants' yoke is being thrown off—except not here in Poland. Like I said, here it's been going in the opposite direction. These Polish-German noblemen are in command of a new feudal system that pretty well makes slaves of their peasant workers."

"Slaves!" cried Bettje. "Are you saying that Count Frankfurt considers us his slaves?"

"Sort of, yes," Mother said quietly.

"But he didn't buy us! How can he claim us as slaves?" protested Bettje.

Mother gave her a look. "Think about it. We're totally dependent on Count Frankfurt—totally at his mercy. Why shouldn't he consider us his slaves? We belong to a sect that is despised all across the face of Europe. Were it not for the Count's protection, we would have fallen into the hands of the Emperor Charles."

Bettje sat silent. After a while she said lamely, "I thought the Count seems quite tolerant of—of different religions."

"He is that," Mother agreed. "Poland as a whole is more tolerant. There is not so much the mindset that the whole country must have the same religion. Poland has Catholics, Lutherans, Eastern Orthodox...even some Muslims where the Turks have gained a foothold. So another 'sect,' as Count Frankfurt calls us, makes no difference to him. And that," Mother concluded, "is why there is only one thing for us to do. Slaves or not, we gratefully accept the haven afforded us on this estate."

"It isn't fair," Bettje muttered.

"Jesus never promised that things would be fair. Look how He was treated while on earth. His own people ended up putting Him on the cross. And recently, Father showed me a verse in the Apostle Paul's first letter to the Corinthians, where Paul says that the followers of Christ are made as the filth of the world, and are the offscouring of all things unto this day' (I Cor.4:13)," Mother related.

There it was again. Mother always seemed to take for granted that Bettje was sympathetic to the brethren's way of life. What if Mother knew how rebellious she felt? Did Mother have any idea how much she hated this life of drudgery in a foreign land, or how greatly she sometimes longed to be back in the "old days" of Leeuwarden?

How Bettje longed to speak with her good friend Lisa again! Yes, there had been betrayal and disappointment—but the memory of Lisa refused to go away. Sometimes Bettje allowed herself to dream of a day when she could escape this cold, damp castle and somehow make her way back to the Leeuwarden she had loved.

Of course Carla, Hannah and the other girls were good friends too. But often Bettje had the sense of not quite belonging. After all, the other girls her age were baptized. They probably didn't struggle anymore with the kind of doubts that plagued her. They always seemed so cheerful and contented and—well, just plain good! As if they didn't mind being called the "offscouring of the world."

Maybe the Apostle Paul thought people should live like that. But Bettje Weaver, formerly of Leeuwarden, was one person who couldn't quite accept being the offscouring of the world!

Unaware of her daughter's turbulent thoughts, Mother was saying, "Count Frankfurt has urged Father to write the Dutch brethren, inviting more of them to come."

"Oh? So he wants more slaves?" Bettje asked sarcastically.

Mother's brow furrowed. "We should look at it this way: the Count wishes to offer asylum to some more of the persecuted brethren."

Though Bettje didn't say it, she doubted whether that was the Count's motivation.

Now the other servants returned to the kitchen, having set the table in the great hall. "The men are coming in for supper," one servant girl announced. "Let's carry the food to the hall."

A long plank table had been set up in the large room where, years ago, the lord of the castle used to hold feasts. Now the workers filed in, their coats dusted with snow and their faces ruddy from the cold. Though their boots were crusted with half-frozen mud and their hands were chapped and raw, they seemed a merry lot as they took seats at the table.

Tonight there was roasted venison from a deer Jan had shot with his bow and arrow. There was also a great platter of fish that the younger boys had caught in the Vistula. Count Frankfurt's worries about his food supply had vanished once he realized what good hunters and fishers these people were.

Weary as usual, Bettje remained seated on the bench after the meal. Enviously she watched the other girls carrying dishes to the kitchen. Even after a long day's work, they did not seem very tired at all.

Jan, too, stayed sitting on the bench. After the other boys had gone off to their sleeping rooms, he edged closer to his sister. Self-consciously he began, "I didn't know if I'd have a chance to be alone with you or not."

Bettje caught her breath. What secret was her brother about to share?

"I was talking with Father while dike building today," he went on in a low voice. "I've asked for baptism. So has Samuel."

"Is—is that so!" Bettje managed. "Well, I—I guess I'm glad for you."

Seriously he replied, "I realized I need to repent and become committed to the will of Christ if I want peace."

"I see," she said again, her voice shaky. Somehow she felt betrayed—and alone.

That night it was a long time before Bettje Weaver fell asleep.

Chapter Twenty-Seven

Ice Dam

The Vistula was not completely covered by ice until the end of January. Only six weeks later, it was already time for the ice to break up. The river's turbulent current strained against its icy prison. Loud cracks and booms punctuated the long, dark February nights.

Yes, that winter the nights were long for Bettje. Often she tossed and turned on her blanket while the hard floor tormented her ribs and questions tormented her mind.

By February, though, one thing was clear to Bettje: she wanted to follow in her brother's footsteps. She, too, wished to be baptized, and take part in the fellowship of the saints.

"Fellowship of the saints." When Father preached, that was one of his favorite sayings. Bettje knew what the Catholics meant by a saint. That was an extra good person, such as Mary the mother of Jesus, or John the apostle.

As far as Bettje could tell, all the brethren considered themselves saints. And that frightened her. How could she ever become a child of God, if she had to be a saint first?

Diligently Bettje listened during the evening Bible studies. She could see that Jan and Samuel were drinking in every word. They wanted to be ready for baptism sometime in the spring. So did Bettje—but she had not told a single soul.

Because first, as far as she could tell, Bettje Weaver would have to become a better person. When God's Word was expounded, she heard so much about goodness and righteousness. Once, Father preached a sermon on the first twelve verses of Matthew 5. "Here is a description of those who enter the kingdom of God," he had said, and then came a whole row of qualifications that seemed far beyond Bettje's reach. Humble, meek, righteous, pure, peaceable and, most unattainable of all, rejoicing in persecution. Those were the children of the kingdom.

Bettje was left in despair. When she looked at her own heart, she saw pride and rebellion. She most definitely did not see a girl who enjoyed persecution! How could she ever be a saint? How could she ever be good enough for baptism?

And so the long nights of tossing and turning went on.

By March, the Vistula's ice was breaking up in earnest. A mighty surge of water from upriver picked up huge rafts of ice and carried them down toward the bay.

"Up in the hills the snow is melting. That's why the water's so high," Father explained. "Count Frankfurt is afraid there'll be an ice jam down near the river's mouth. And that means flooding here!"

"Surely the river won't rise all the way to the castle," Titus exclaimed.

Father responded, "The Count says it's been dangerously close, other years."

Every day the water rose. The river had turned into a lake—a roiling brown lake that lapped up the fields and crept toward the castle.

"Obviously, the ice has dammed the river. The water can't get into the Baltic Sea anymore," Bernhard said.

One night in March the alarm was sounded: all hands were needed to move livestock to higher ground! "Let's go too," Carla urged the other girls who slept in the same room as Bettje. "If nothing else, we could move the chickens and ducks."

Forlornly, Bettje watched her friends go. Even though she was gradually getting better, she knew she would be useless for a task like that. "I'll stay here with you, Anneken and Mary," she said.

The smaller girls soon fell asleep. Wishing she could sleep too, Bettje lay down on her blanket.

Suddenly the heavy door swung open. Were the girls coming back already? Someone moved slowly toward her in the darkness.

"It's just me," came Mother's soothing voice. "I thought I'd keep you company, since nearly everyone has gone out to move the livestock to higher ground."

"With all the sheep, goats, cattle and horses the Count owns, I guess that's quite a chore," Bettje whispered. Sitting on one end of her blanket, she made room for Mother close by. They sat in silence for a while, listening to the rushing water that now lapped at the castle's foundations.

"Bettje, do you remember the Sunday when Herr Bolger and his friends came to our worship meeting for the first time, there in Friesland?" Mother questioned.

"Yes," replied Bettje, wondering why she thought of that.

"Do you remember which miracle of Christ's Father preached about that day?" came Mother's next question.

"I think it was the one where Jesus raised that little girl to life. The daughter of Jairus."

"You have a good memory. Maybe you also recall Father's comments on that story?"

"N-no, not really."

"I remember him saying, 'We need to feel Christ's hand upon us.'

Ice Dam 117

Because, you know, Jesus had taken that maiden's hand before telling her to arise."

"Yes, I remember that."

"Well, Bettje, the last while Father and I have been wondering whether…whether perhaps you are feeling Christ's hand upon you."

Mystified, Bettje asked, "Why do you say that?"

"When people begin seeking the Lord, that is what happens. His hand is upon us. Father and I have such vivid memories of the days and weeks before we surrendered our lives to Jesus. Oh, how tormented our consciences were! We wanted the truth—we wanted peace—but we hardly knew how to attain it. Does that sound familiar to you, Bettje?"

A sob caught in Bettje's throat. To think that her parents understood—and that they had noticed her struggles! "It's just—it's just that I'm afraid I can never be good enough. And yet I want to be a child of God," she said brokenly.

"Oh, Bettje." Mother touched her arm. "Then it's just as Father and I thought. Christ's hand is on you, drawing you. And do you know what Father said I'm to tell you? It's true that Jesus commanded the girl to rise up and walk. But would He have commanded a dead girl to walk? Would He, Bettje?"

"Wh-why, no, I suppose not."

"Of course not! First He gave her life. Then He commanded her to walk—and He gave her the power to do so. We get things mixed up, Bettje. We try to 'walk' when we are still 'dead'—and that doesn't work."

"I don't know what you mean."

"Well, you say you've been trying so hard to be 'good enough.' But that isn't really what Jesus wants. He died to save us from sin. He wants us to believe that. When we see how sinful we are, and then believe that He can save us, we receive new life. That's when we can begin responding to His command to rise up and walk!"

Bettje drew a trembling breath. "Oh. I had it mixed up. I see that now."

"Jesus wants us to surrender. That's a big word, with a big meaning. Probably most of all, surrendering means to stop establishing a righteousness of our own, and instead begin trusting in Christ's righteousness. It makes a difference," Mother assured her. Then she began to pray.

Doors opened. Someone shouted, "Count Frankfurt says everybody has to move to the castle's second floor! At this level the water is coming in!"

So Mother stopped praying and quickly asked, "You want to surrender, don't you, Bettje?"

"Yes, I do," Bettje replied feelingly. Then she picked up her blanket and went to rouse little Mary. Mother took Anneken's hand, and together they began climbing the long flight of stone steps.

Strangely, in spite of the water's roar and people's frantic cries, Bettje's heart lilted with the words of a hymn: "Peace, be still. Peace, be still."

Nearby in the darkness a child asked, "Will the river carry the castle away too?"

And a mother replied, "I don't think so. This castle has a strong foundation built of stone."

Bettje smiled to herself as she sat down and wrapped her blanket around her. Like that "cleft in the rock," this castle was high and safe above the threatening waves.

Later, after the castle had gone quiet, Bettje prayed her own prayer. It was a prayer of repentance, and of faith so new that it trembled—but it was faith nevertheless.

Chapter Twenty-Eight

Incorruptible Seed

The next morning when Bettje looked out beyond the wide stone casement, angry brown water was everywhere. All the barns were half-submerged. Only the roofs of the tenant houses showed above the water.

"Did all the peasants reach safety?" Bettje asked in concern.

"As far as I know, they were alerted in time," Carla replied. "Some are here in the castle. Others fled up the hill with the cattle."

Eastward, where the rising sun sent up strong red rays, Bettje could see the cattle and horses on a high slope. "Are the chickens and ducks up there too?" she wondered.

"Yes. The ducks will be all right, I'm sure—but I'm a little worried about the chickens," Carla admitted. "If they don't know enough to go up higher when the water rises, they will drown by the dozens."

Bettje cocked an ear. "The sheep and cattle must be hungry. I hear them bleating and lowing."

"There's really no food for them up there. And I suppose much of the hay in the barns is all soggy now. I hope this flood goes down soon, so the grass in the fields can start growing," Carla fretted.

That evening, the water began to subside. Faster and faster it surged, as though swirling down a huge drain. Bettje could not tear her eyes from the "disappearing lake." Before darkness fell, most of the fields had emerged from beneath the water. Obviously, the ice jam had broken up, freeing the river to once again empty into the bay.

In the following days, spring came in earnest. By April there were some dry fields, and the eager sowers could begin to cast their seed.

"How precious it is when God's Word is sown in tender hearts, and new life springs forth," Father said during his sermon on the day of baptism. "In I Peter 1 we read that we are 'born again, not of corruptible seed, but of incorruptible, by the word of God, which liveth and abideth forever.' So to you dear souls who have trusted in Jesus—as long as you stay faithful, you have growing in your bosom something of the eternal. No matter if the world sends raging floods of affliction—the Word of God 'liveth and abideth forever.'"

Sitting there in the cow shed with the others who sought baptism, Bettje pictured the great flood that had covered the Count's fields. Now there was dry soil, and the first green shoots were poking through to the sunlight.

How meaningful the Bible study meetings had been for Bettje during the weeks just past! In the winter, a fog seemed to hover around the explanations of the brethren. Now the fog had lifted. Trusting in the righteousness of the One who had come to dwell in her heart, Bettje longed to wholly submit her life to Jesus.

In all, thirteen people received baptism that day. Lately some peasant families had been coming to the worship and Bible study meetings, and now two sets of parents were being baptized, along with some young people. Truly it was happening as Father had said when they planned to leave Leeuwarden: "We will carry the truth to other lands and cause the church to grow."

On the afternoon of the baptismal service, the Weaver family—along with the Claessens, of course—gathered in one of the castle rooms. With a happy sigh Father said to Mother, "Three more of our children now take part in the fellowship of the saints."

Bettje glanced over at Jan and Samuel. Yes, the Claessen children were so much a part of the family that Father could speak of Samuel as his son.

But that phrase about the "fellowship of the saints" reminded Bettje of some questions. Quickly, before she lost courage, she asked, "What is the Bible meaning of 'saint'?"

"'Saint' comes from the word 'save,'" Father answered promptly. "A saint is a 'saved one'—a person called out of the world into the kingdom of God."

"Ooh," said Bettje as understanding dawned.

Father's eyes were still upon her. "Were you perhaps thinking of 'saints' as the Catholics view them—people deserving of our adoration?"

"I guess I was," admitted Bettje.

"Such a corrupted view is far from the Bible's simplicity. No humans are worthy of adoration. As God's 'saved ones,' our adoration belongs wholly to the One who saves us!"

Locking his hands behind his head, Father leaned back against the wall. "Today I kept thinking of Captain Nordstrom and his crew. In fact, several times this morning I cast a glance downriver, hoping to see a boat with them aboard."

"You mean because some of them seemed so close to the kingdom last fall?" queried Mother.

Father nodded. "Abel had the beginnings of faith. Fruits were showing. Remember how he heaped coals of fire on the pirates' heads?"

Adam recalled smilingly, "He even gave away his shoes."

"Abel planned to spend the winter in Gdansk. Before we left his ship, I encouraged him to come upriver to our meetings. But he never came." Father's voice was sad. "It is a painful thing when a man is so close to the kingdom—yet refuses to make that full surrender. No doubt the call of worldly commerce claimed Abel this spring. He has probably laden his ship with goods and is halfway across the Baltic by now."

Father paused, then quoted with lingering sadness these words from the gospel of Matthew: 'For what is a man profited, if he shall gain the whole world, and lose his own soul? or what shall a man give in exchange for his soul?'" (Matt.16:26).

Chapter Twenty-Nine

Lisa, Too

From the castle window, Bettje gazed unhappily down over the garden. Out there were most of her friends, busily planting rows and rows of seeds. In fact, Carla, Hannah and Gertrude were working in the grain fields today. Seed bags slung over their shoulders, they swung their arms, broadcasting rye and oats. Most of the men were so busy with drainage projects that the Count had asked for some girls to help plant the fields.

Turning from the window, Bettje burst out, "Mother, why can't I just get well, instead of dragging on and on with this illness? I'm so tired of—of being tired all the time."

"We must be patient. We're hoping that once you can eat fresh fruits and vegetables from the garden, you will quickly get better."

Mother's voice, though kind, also carried a hint of reproach. A stab went through Bettje. She scolded herself, "There I go, complaining again. Why do I complain so much? Surely a child of God should not be so easily discouraged."

For some days now, such thoughts had been bothering Bettje. Where was all this righteousness that was supposed to spring up in the believer's life? Indeed, where was her newness of life? All too often, Bettje struggled with the same old thoughts and feelings of former days.

I wonder what is wrong with me, Bettje thought miserably as she helped Mother prepare turnips for that evening's stew. Thump, thump, went her knife on the cutting board. Every now and then, a turnip had a rotten spot. Considering that only a few weeks ago, the whole cellar had been flooded, it was no wonder that the turnips were spoiling.

I'm like a no-good turnip, needing to be trimmed, Bettje's thoughts went on. At last she reminded herself, *Why don't I tell Mother about my struggles? Last winter I'd have saved myself a lot of trouble by talking to her sooner.*

Sharing wasn't easy. Inside Bettje lurked something—pride, perhaps?—that would rather have put up a front and pretended there was nothing wrong. But why miss such a good chance, when she was alone in the kitchen with Mother?

Bettje cleared her throat. "Mother, I wish I wouldn't complain so much. I repent and ask for forgiveness, but then it happens again. I guess I'm not much of a—a saint."

Mother turned to look at her. "One of the marks of a saint is that he mourns his own failings and weaknesses."

"Huh?" After a moment of puzzled silence, Bettje exclaimed, "Are you saying any believer will feel that way? But you others seem so much better than I. You don't look like you're struggling with—with sin."

"Sometimes we do, though. Just because we are saved by the blood of Christ doesn't mean our old nature can no longer cause trouble. You know what, Bettje? I wish we could discuss this with Father. Why don't we go out and see whether he's working on our house?

He sometimes grabs a few minutes shortly before suppertime for that project. I know he really hopes to have a house ready for us by winter."

Together they walked from the castle toward the tenant houses. To their right, the Vistula flowed broad and calm between greening banks. Bettje shaded her eyes to gaze downriver. "There's a boat coming this way," she remarked.

Mother did not reply. At this time of year boats were a common sight on the Vistula.

Sure enough, when Bettje and Mother came to the new house, Father was hammering away at the frame. The men had gone up to the forests and floated down some logs; now a number of new tenant houses were springing up. Castle life was okay for a while, but the families all longed for homes of their own.

"Bettje had some questions about why she still struggles with failings and weaknesses," Mother began. "I wanted her to hear what you would say to that."

Sitting on a squared timber, Father began using an adze to pare away thin shavings of wood. "Remember how I've sometimes compared God's salvation plan to the reclamation of boggy land?"

Bettje sat down on the other end of the log. "You used that for an illustration back when you first told us how you and Mother became believers."

"That's right, I did. I suggested that the earth at creation was like a big marshy bog. Then God caused the dry land to appear, where plants could grow and fruit could spring forth. But as we learned in Bible study this spring, man fell into sin. The heart of man became permeated with sin, like a marshy bog. However, through Jesus, God has reclaimed the world from the power of sin!

"When you repent of your sinful nature and believe in Jesus, something similar happens on a personal level. God has reclaimed your heart, away from the power of sin, to bear fruit for Him.

"But Bettje, think about it. Reclaiming is an ongoing thing. We must stay at work, digging ditches, building and repairing dikes. We must plow and plant and weed if we want to see fruits.

"When we believe, we say that we are saved—reclaimed. And that is true, on God's side. But for us there is a kind of 'saving' or 'reclaiming' that has to continue day by day all our life long. And that's why there's such a thing as struggles in the life of the believer." With a smile, Father looked up from his work. "Does that help you understand, Bettje?"

"Yes. Thank you." Turning to look at the river, Bettje caught her breath. "That boat is tying up at the Frankfurt dock! I wonder who it could be?"

"Shall we walk down there?" Mother suggested.

"Let's." Bettje saw the guards striding to the dock. She could imagine their stern question, "Who comes here?"

Father commented, "Something about the people in the boat makes me think they're refugees."

"Maybe it's someone we know!" exclaimed Bettje. "You did send a letter to Obbe Phillips in Leeuwarden to let him know that the Count would welcome more workers."

Now the refugees—if such they were—clambered out of the boat. Even from a distance they were a sorry-looking lot.

"Their clothes are in tatters," Bettje whispered. "Is that how we looked when we came?"

Suddenly Bettje began running. She had not run for months. But she was running now, and from her lips burst a single name, over and over: "Lisa! Lisa!"

For this gaunt, hollow-eyed girl in a soiled cloak and bedraggled skirt was none other than her friend Lisa of Leeuwarden.

Their hands locked, and for a moment they stared at one another, speechless. A depth of sadness in her friend's eyes made Bettje glance quickly over the group. Lisa's parents were not there.

Lisa, Too

Before Bettje could ask, Lisa whispered painfully, "They were executed."

"For their faith? Were they—are you—?" Bettje stopped herself, Why else would Lisa be here?

Tears spilled over Lisa's cheeks. "They trusted in Jesus. Before we could flee, the authorities took them."

"And you? Are you—?" Again, Bettje couldn't bring herself to ask the question.

"I too have been baptized. How could I bear the sadness, if it were not for Jesus?"

Impulsively, Bettje took Lisa's hand again. "Then we are sisters," she said.